Exile: The Mortal Chronicles of Vasuki

Aayush Aggarwal

Printed in India

IndiePress

ISBN: 978-93-6045-959-8

First Printing, 2025

IndiePress

A division of Nasadiya Technologies Private Ltd.

Koramangala, Bangalore

Karnataka-560029

http://indiepress.in/

Edited by Ridham Bassi

Typeset by Zoheb Ahmed

Book Cover designed by Nikhil Kamath

Publishing Consultant – Zoheb Ahmed

Contents

अनन्तं वासुकिं सेषं पद्मनाभं च कम्बलम्

संखपालं धर्तराष्ट्रं तक्षकं कलियं तथा

एतानि नव नमानि नगणमा च महात्मनम्

सायामकले पथेन्नित्यं प्रतक्कले विषेषतः

तस्य विशभयं नस्ति सर्वत्र विजयी भवेत

anantam vasukim sesham padmanabham cha kambalam

samkhpalam dhartarashtram takshakam kaliyam tatha

etani nava namani naganama cha mahatmanam

saayamakale pathennityam pratakkale viseshatah

tasya vishabhayam nasti sarvatra vijayi bhaveth

Chapter 1: The Awakening of Vasuki

The desert sun beat down on the old temple of Chandravati, casting long shadows over the worn sandstone walls and broken pillars. Two workers, Suraj and Manu, stopped to wipe the sweat from their faces. They rested for a moment, leaning on their shovels, taking shade under a crumbling pillar.

The old Chandravati temple complex stretched out over the empty desert like a sleeping giant. Its once-grand buildings were now just worn ruins. The air around it was filled with the quiet sounds of history, telling tales of people and places that had been lost for a long time.

"Have you seen Dr. Nair today?" Suraj asked, glancing toward the entrance of the site. Manu nodded, a look of admiration crossing his face. "Oh, yes. He arrived just before dawn, as usual. Always the first one here and the last one to leave." Suraj smiled. "He's a hard worker, that one. They say he's one of the best archaeologists in the country." Manu nodded again, more vigorously this time. “And not just in India. People talk about him all over the world. You know, my cousin works at another site in Rajasthan, and he told me that Dr. Nair once found an entire underground city. Can you imagine?” Suraj’s eyes widened. “An underground city? No wonder he’s so respected.”

Right then, the man they were talking about showed up at the edge of the dig site. When he was in his early forties, Dr. Vikram Nair was both intimidating and friendly. On his head, a wide-brimmed hat blocked the sun from his dark, wavy hair. He wore khaki pants and a clean white shirt that was starting to get dirty. His thin but strong body showed how hard his work in the field was on his body.

Suraj elbowed Manu lightly. “There he is. Speak of the devil.” Manu watched as Vikram made his way toward them, his strides confident and purposeful. “Do you know what I admire most about him?” Manu asked, not waiting for an answer. “It’s his dedication. He’s always so focused, so passionate about uncovering the past.” Suraj nodded in agreement. “And he’s respectful too. He treats us like we’re all part of the team, not just laborers.”

Vikram walked up to the two men and looked around the spot with a trained eye. A hint of his white teeth stood out against his tanned skin in his friendly smile when he saw them. “Good morning, Suraj and Manu, *Kaisa chal raha hai kaam? Sab theek*?” Vikram greeted them in fluent Hindi, his voice carrying both authority and kindness. “How are we progressing today?” “We’ve made good progress on the west side, Dr. Nair,” Suraj replied, standing a bit straighter. “But we hit some large rocks that are slowing us down.” Vikram nodded thoughtfully. “Those rocks could be significant. They might be part of a collapsed structure. Let's make sure we document everything carefully before we move them." Manu, always eager to contribute, chimed in. "Dr. Nair, we found some pottery shards near the rocks. They look different from what we've seen so far." Vikram's eyes lit up with interest. "Show me."

The two laborers led Vikram to the area where they had been working. He knelt down, examining the shards with practiced expertise. "These are indeed different," he mused. "The design is unique—this could indicate a different period or even a different culture." He looked up at Suraj and Manu, his expression serious but encouraging. "You both have done excellent work. Keep at it, and remember to document everything meticulously. Every piece, no matter how small, helps us understand the bigger picture."

Suraj and Manu exchanged proud smiles. "Yes, Dr. Nair," they said in unison. Vikram stood, dusting off his hands. "I'll be nearby if you need me. Let's uncover history together." As Vikram walked away to join Anjali and the rest of the team, Suraj turned to Manu with a grin. "See? That's why he's the best. Not just because he's brilliant, but because he respects and values everyone's contribution." Manu nodded, a sense of pride swelling in his chest. "We're lucky to be part of this team."

The two workers went back to work with more energy after seeing how dedicated and respected their boss was. Vikram became interested in history and archaeology at a young age. He was born into a family of teachers. His thesis at Oxford University was about the ancient civilizations of the Indian subcontinent, which won him his PhD. Vikram's job has taken him to some of the most remote and historically important places in the world. He is known for his careful study methods and unwavering dedication.

"*Sambhaalkar,*" Vikram called out in fluent Hindi, his voice carrying authority laced with respect for the ruins. "We must preserve everything intact. Every fragment here holds the potential to unlock the mysteries of our past."

A group of archaeologists and local workers moved around him with disciplined speed. They moved in sync with each other like a well-choreographed dance while the sands moved in the background. Vikram's trusted coworker, Dr. Anjali Kapoor, was one of them. She was smart and dedicated all the time. Anjali was in her late thirties, thin, and had her dark hair pulled back into a sensible bun. Vikram could always count on her as a coworker.

Anjali came from a family of scholars and grew up surrounded by books and artifacts. She specialized in ancient languages and inscriptions, earning praise for her work in translating and interpreting texts from old sites. Her expertise and attention to detail made her a valuable member of any archaeological team.

The temple complex lay before them, its worn sandstone walls covered with detailed carvings from a long-lost civilization. As the team moved further into the site, Vikram's excitement grew. This wasn't just an excavation—it was a journey into history, a mission to uncover secrets hidden under centuries of sand and neglect.

Anjali knelt beside a newly uncovered section of the temple wall, gently brushing off the dust. The carvings beneath showed scenes of myths and legends—gods and mortals locked in eternal struggle. "Vikram," she called out, her voice tinged with excitement, "Come take a look at this." Vikram quickly moved over, his curiosity sparked. He knelt beside Anjali, studying the glyphs and symbols on the ancient stone. The carvings showed scenes from forgotten myths, a reminder of a civilization lost to time.

"These inscriptions are remarkable," Anjali remarked, her voice barely above a whisper. "They speak of a time when gods and mortals walked side by side when legends were born, and empires rose and fell." Vikram nodded thoughtfully, his fingertips tracing the contours of the carvings with a mixture of awe and scholarly reverence. "Indeed," he agreed. "These carvings could provide invaluable insights into the beliefs and practices of the ancient civilization that once thrived here."

As the team worked hard to document every detail, Vikram's mind raced with possibilities. He had dedicated his life to uncovering the mysteries of the past, driven by a strong desire for knowledge and a need to reveal truths buried under time and neglect. "Keep digging," Vikram instructed the team, his voice tinged with excitement. "There's more to uncover here—secrets that have lain dormant for centuries."

The sun climbed higher in the sky as the excavation continued, casting long shadows across the ancient ruins. The air buzzed with anticipation as each discovery brought them closer to understanding the enigma of Chandravati and its significance in the annals of history.

Little did Vikram know that their greatest discovery lay just beneath the sands, waiting to be unearthed—a relic of immense power and ancient wisdom that would forever alter the course of their lives.

The air was thick with anticipation as the team worked tirelessly to uncover the mysteries buried beneath centuries of sand and neglect. Vikram Nair, his dark eyes ablaze with scholarly fervor, led the excavation with precision and determination. Beside him, Dr. Anjali Kapoor, a woman of sharp intellect and unwavering dedication, offered invaluable insights into the ancient carvings that adorned the temple walls.

As the excavation continued, Vikram's mind raced with possibilities. He had dedicated his life to unraveling the mysteries of the past, driven by an insatiable thirst for knowledge and a deep-seated desire to uncover truths hidden beneath layers of time and neglect.

The excavation site was alive with activity, filled with the sound of scraping tools and quiet chatter as the team uncovered fragments of the past. At the center, Vikram focused on the temple's intricate carvings, rich with ancient stories. Beside him, Dr. Anjali Kapoor carefully cataloged artifacts, her keen mind unraveling the mystery of Chandravati's history.The sun rose higher as the excavation went on, casting long shadows over the ruins. The air was filled with anticipation, each new discovery bringing them closer to understanding the mystery of Chandravati and its place in history.

What Vikram didn't know was that their greatest find was just beneath the sands, waiting to be uncovered—a relic of great power and ancient wisdom that would change their lives forever.

The team worked tirelessly to uncover the secrets buried beneath centuries of neglect. Vikram, his eyes full of passion, led the excavation with care and determination.

Beside him, Dr. Anjali Kapoor, with her sharp intellect and dedication, provided key insights into the ancient carvings on the temple walls.

As the work continued, Vikram's mind raced with possibilities. His life had been spent searching for the truths hidden in the past, driven by a thirst for knowledge and a desire to reveal the secrets of time.

Suddenly, a commotion disrupted their work. Excited voices from the far end of the site caught Vikram and Anjali's attention. They exchanged a glance and rushed over. Among the rubble, a faint glimmer of polished metal reflected the sunlight. Vikram's heart raced as he called out, "Bring the brushes."

Vikram called out, his voice steady but edged with urgency. "We need to see this clearly." As the workers cleared away the last bits of sand and debris, Anjali Kapoor, just as intrigued, joined Vikram at the edge of the pit where the artifact was half-buried. She carefully used a small brush to sweep away the remaining sand. Vikram knelt beside the artifact, brushing off the sand with steady hands. Slowly, the artifact began to emerge, and a gasp of awe spread through the team. It was a stunning serpentine figure made of ancient bronze, about two feet tall. The artifact showed a coiled serpent, its body twisting with both power and grace. The delicate details and shimmering surface gave it an otherworldly, captivating beauty.

"It's a serpent," Anjali whispered, her voice filled with awe.

Chandravati was rich in mythology. It was believed to be the home of Vasuki, the divine serpent, and many thought the temple complex held the secret to ancient wisdom and supernatural powers. "But look at the details, Vikram. It's unlike anything we've seen before." Vikram nodded, his eyes filled with amazement. The craftsmanship was extraordinary. Each scale on the serpent was carefully detailed, making it seem like the creature could come to life at any moment. The bronze had a worn, greenish-brown color, showing its age and ancient roots. Even after all these years, the artifact still had a mysterious shine, as if something invisible was guarding it.

The serpent's head was the most impressive part. It appeared ready to strike, its mouth open to show sharp, detailed fangs. Its eyes were set with small, sparkling emerald gemstones that seemed to glow from within. These eyes were captivating, pulling viewers in and evoking a feeling of awe and respect.

Along the serpent's body, there were several inscriptions in a script that Vikram and Anjali recognized but couldn't immediately understand. The symbols seemed to combine ancient languages, hinting that the artifact could have been a sacred artifact in a forgotten civilization. The base was a solid, circular piece of bronze, engraved with more symbols—likely a mantra or spell to channel the serpent's power. It was clear that the artifact was designed for both artistic and ritualistic purposes.

Upon closer inspection, Vikram noticed tiny, nearly invisible channels along the serpent's body. These channels suggested a hidden mechanism, possibly a way to release something or reveal a secret compartment. The idea fascinated Vikram, sparking his curiosity to uncover the artifact's mysteries. "This craftsmanship is extraordinary," Vikram murmured, tracing his finger along the serpent's sinuous curves. "Every scale ... it's as if the artist breathed life into the bronze." Anjali glanced at him, a smile playing on her lips. "You always know how to find the poetry in these discoveries." He met her gaze, a soft smile forming. "And you always know how to decipher their secrets."

The artifact seemed to radiate an energy that commanded both respect and curiosity. It was more than just a work of art; it was a symbol of a civilization that held the serpent as a representation of power, wisdom, and mystery. As Vikram and Anjali stood before it, they felt as though they were on the verge of a groundbreaking discovery—one that could change history and reshape their understanding of the ancient world.

"Those eyes," Anjali said, leaning in closer. "They almost look alive. I've never seen gemstones set so perfectly." As Vikram and Anjali continued to examine the artifact, other members of the team gathered around, their curiosity piqued. Raj, a young archaeologist with a keen interest in ancient scripts, knelt beside Anjali and Vikram. "Look at these inscriptions," Raj pointed out, his voice tinged with excitement. Vikram glanced at Raj, appreciating his enthusiasm. "Raj, what do you make of these inscriptions?" Raj leaned in closer, his fingers tracing the symbols etched along the serpent's body. "They seem to be a mix of ancient languages. I recognize some elements of Brahmi script, but there are other symbols here that I've never seen before. This could be a significant find, perhaps even a key to understanding more about the civilization that created this." Vikram nodded, his mind racing. "We need to document everything. Anjali, can you start sketching the inscriptions? Raj, get the camera and start taking detailed photographs."

As Anjali began sketching the serpent's details, she looked up. "Do you think you can decipher it?" Raj nodded, his mind already racing with possibilities. "It will take time, but I'm confident we can make progress. These inscriptions could provide invaluable insights." As Raj began photographing the artifact, his excitement was palpable. "We need to document every detail meticulously. This could rewrite what we know about ancient Indian history." Vikram nodded in agreement, feeling a surge of pride in his team's dedication. "Let's get to work, then. There's something more here." Vikram knew that the walls of Chandravati were a canvas of history. "The more we uncover, the closer we get to understanding the true significance of this artifact," Vikram said thoughtfully. "These channels might indicate a hidden compartment or a mechanism. We need to be very careful in our examination."

The base of the artifact was a solid piece of bronze, circular and inscribed with more symbols. Vikram knelt to get a closer look, feeling a strange sense of connection to the artifact. "This base," he said, tracing the symbols with his fingertips. "It could be an incantation or a mantra—something meant to harness the serpent's power."

Hours went by as the team carefully documented their findings, with the sun setting in the background. Raj's camera clicked constantly, capturing every angle and detail of the artifact. His mind was focused on the symbols and their possible meanings, his academic curiosity sparking an intense determination to uncover the truth.

As the team carefully documented every detail, the air was filled with excitement and reverence. The artifact seemed to exude an energy that demanded both respect and curiosity. "Do you think it's a symbol of worship?" Anjali asked, her eyes still fixed on the serpent's hypnotic gaze. "Possibly," Vikram replied. "Or perhaps a representation of something even more significant. We need to dig deeper—literally and figuratively—to understand its true purpose."

"We've made a remarkable discovery today," Vikram said, addressing the team. "But this is just the beginning. Let's secure the artifact and continue our work. There's so much more to uncover." Vikram placed a reassuring hand on Raj's shoulder. "Excellent work today, Raj. This is just the beginning. Your expertise will be crucial in deciphering these inscriptions."

Raj smiled, feeling the weight of the responsibility and the thrill of discovery. "I won't let you down, Vikram. This artifact holds secrets we're only beginning to uncover."

As the team carefully lifted the artifact from its resting place, Raj couldn't shake the feeling that their discovery would lead to something monumental—something that would challenge everything they knew about history, identity, and the line between myth and reality. Vikram shared that sense of anticipation, knowing this discovery would set off a chain of events that would alter their understanding of history and the very fabric of reality itself.

"It's breathtaking," Anjali breathed, her voice filled with awe. "Do you think … ?" Vikram nodded slowly, his gaze fixed on the artifact. "I believe so. This could be more than just a relic of the past. It could be a key to unlocking the mysteries that have eluded us for centuries."

As they examined the artifact, Vikram felt a subtle shift within himself—a stirring of ancient memories long buried. Images flashed in his mind, brief glimpses of a distant past wrapped in myth and legend. He felt a deep connection to the artifact, an unexplainable bond that went beyond scholarly curiosity.

Anjali nodded in agreement, her brow furrowed in concentration. "We need to document every detail," she said firmly. "This could rewrite history as we know it."

Hours passed in a blur as Vikram and his team carefully documented every detail of the artifact and its surroundings. The artifact seemed to pulse with an energy that couldn't be explained, its presence captivating everyone and filling the air with fascination and intrigue.

As the sun dipped below the horizon, casting long shadows across the temple ruins, Vikram made a quiet promise to unravel the artifact's mysteries, regardless of the cost. Little did he know, their discovery would set off a chain of events that would shake his very understanding of history, identity, and the boundary between myth and reality.

Unknown to his team, Vikram felt a quiet shift within himself—a stirring of long-forgotten ancient memories. He sensed a deep connection to the artifact, an unexplainable bond that went beyond academic curiosity. Fleeting images of a distant past, shrouded in myth and legend, flashed through his mind.

Time passed quickly as Vikram and his team carefully documented every detail of the artifact and its surroundings. As the sun set, casting long shadows across the temple ruins, Vikram silently vowed to uncover the artifact's secrets, no matter the cost. He had no idea that this discovery would trigger events that would challenge everything he believed about history, identity, and the line between myth and reality.

As the sun dipped lower, Vikram's determination grew stronger. The bronze serpent, with its detailed carvings and mysterious aura, seemed to hold secrets that called to him.

Anjali, noticing Vikram's pensive mood, approached him. "Are you alright, Vikram? You seem ... distant." Vikram forced a smile, though his mind was elsewhere. "I'm fine, Anjali. Just thinking about everything we've uncovered. There's something about this artifact that feels ... personal." Anjali nodded, her expression thoughtful. "I feel it, too. It's as if the artifact is alive, carrying the weight of its history and the souls that revered it." Raj joined them, holding his notebook filled with sketches and notes. "The inscriptions are unlike anything I've ever seen. They tell a story, but it's fragmented. We need to piece it together." Maya, who had been setting up the camp for the night, added, "We've documented everything thoroughly. Whatever secrets this artifact holds, we'll find them." Rohan, tinkering with his scanner, glanced up. "I've managed to capture every detail of the artifact. Once we analyze the data, we might find something we've missed."

Maya, a historian focused on ancient mythologies and their modern relevance, met Vikram at an archaeology conference and was intrigued by his research. Rohan, an engineer with an interest in technology and the supernatural, joined Vikram's team because of his passion for ancient artifacts. He brought technical expertise and a healthy dose of skepticism, balancing Maya's academic approach with practical insights into the artifact's possible technological aspects.

Vikram looked at his team, and their dedication and enthusiasm were evident. "We've come this far together.

Let's rest tonight and start fresh in the morning. We have a lot of work ahead of us."

The next morning, the team gathered around the artifact, ready to delve deeper into its mysteries. Vikram began by carefully examining the serpent, tracing the intricate patterns with his fingers. As he did, the images from his dreams—the flashes of a distant past—became more vivid. "Look here," Vikram said, pointing to a series of small symbols hidden within the larger design. "These might be the key to understanding the artifact's true purpose." Anjali leaned in, her eyes narrowing as she studied the symbols. "They resemble an ancient script, one that predates any known civilization. If we can translate this, we might uncover the artifact's origin." Raj flipped through his notes, comparing the symbols to other ancient scripts. "It's a complex language, but I think I see a pattern. These symbols could represent elements of nature—earth, water, fire, air." Maya, always the practical one, suggested, "If the symbols represent elements, maybe they're part of a ritual or incantation—something that binds the artifact's power." Rohan, scanning the symbols with his device, added, "There's definitely an energy signature here. It's faint, but it's consistent with what we experienced during the trial."

Vikram nodded, his mind racing. "We need to decipher these symbols and understand their significance. It's the only way to unlock the artifact's full potential."

Days turned into weeks as the team immersed themselves in their research. They compared the symbols to ancient texts, consulted experts, and ran countless tests. Each discovery brought them closer to the truth but also raised new questions.

One day, in a dimly lit camp, Vikram, Anjali, Maya, Rohan, and Raj gathered around the artifact. The room was filled with ancient manuscripts, artifacts, and digital screens displaying scans of the artifacts from various angles. "These symbols … they're more than just ornamental. They seem to form a narrative," said Vikram, examining the artifact closely. Anjali, leaning in and studying the inscriptions, added, "Indeed. Look here; these hieroglyphs resemble those found in ancient texts related to Vasuki. Could this artifact be depicting Vasuki's journey?" Raj, scrutinizing a digital scan, interjected, "I've compared these symbols with those found in the ruins at Chandravati. There's coherence in their sequence. It's as if each symbol tells a part of a larger story." Maya, cross-referencing with her notes, remarked, "The serpent motif here … it's consistent with Vasuki's iconography. But why depict his story in this artifact?" Rohan, adjusting his glasses and analyzing data, suggested, "From a technological standpoint, these symbols might not just be symbolic but could encode information. We need to decipher their meaning to understand their narrative." Vikram, nodding thoughtfully, concluded, "If these symbols are indeed telling Vasuki's story, it could shed light on his purpose for living among humans. It might reveal insights into his experiences and motivations." Anjali added, "Perhaps Vasuki's presence among mortals isn't just a mythological tale. This artifact could be a record of his interactions and influence over ancient civilizations." Maya chimed in, "And if that's true, it could reshape our understanding of mythology and history. We might be on the verge of uncovering a pivotal moment in human-divine interactions." Raj cautioned, "But deciphering these symbols won't be easy. It requires a deep understanding of Vasuki's mythology and the context of these civilizations." Rohan proposed, "I can develop a software algorithm to analyze the patterns and sequences. It might help us decode the narrative structure embedded in these symbols." Vikram encouraged, "Good. Let's combine our expertise. Anjali, continue translating the inscriptions. Maya, gather all references to Vasuki's mythological encounters. Rohan, work on that algorithm. Raj and I will delve deeper into the archaeological context."

The team continued their discussion late into the night, analyzing the artifact's symbols and their meaning. Each member contributed a unique perspective, combining mythology, linguistics, technology, and archaeology. As they uncovered the symbolism, a clearer picture of Vasuki's story took shape, revealing him as not just a mythical figure but a complex part of ancient civilizations.

Their discovery marked a turning point in both their research and their understanding of Vasuki's role in history. It suggested deeper truths waiting to be uncovered and highlighted the artifact's potential to change scholarly perspectives.

Chapter 2: Unveiling the Past

Mount Mandara stood as a giant in the center of the celestial realm, its peak reaching into the heavens. An ancient mountain, it was linked to the creation of the universe. The air around it was filled with a peaceful yet powerful energy, shaped by countless prayers and divine commands over the ages.

The slopes of Mount Mandara were covered in vibrant gardens where plants of every color thrived. Flowers glowed with an inner light, and trees bore fruits of knowledge and wisdom, each plant serving a purpose beyond beauty. Crystal-clear streams flowed down the mountain, their waters creating a peaceful, soothing sound.

At the top of the sacred mountain stood the celestial halls, a grand structure where the divine gathered. The halls were a masterpiece made from materials found only in the divine realm. Walls of glowing crystal reflected the colors of the cosmos, filling the chamber with a beautiful, shifting light.

Pillars of pure quartz rose to the ceiling, each carved with symbols and runes that told of the cosmos' creation and the gods' wisdom. The floor, a mosaic of celestial gemstones, shimmered with every step, reflecting the light from above. In the center of the hall was a large, circular platform inscribed with symbols of balance and harmony, representing the unity of the divine assembly.

The ceiling of the celestial hall was a stunning dome of clear crystal, offering a view of the vast universe. Stars and constellations moved slowly, their patterns shifting to reflect the cosmic order. This dome reminded the divine assembly of the endlessness of creation and allowed them to observe and influence the mortal world below.

The air in the hall hummed softly, resonating with the combined energy of the deities. The atmosphere was peaceful yet full of power, reflecting the presence of the divine beings.

At the far end of the hall were the thrones of the gods, raised on a platform of light. Each throne was unique, symbolizing the essence and dominion of its occupant: Indra, Saraswati, and Agastya.

Goddess Saraswati's throne was a symbol of elegance and wisdom. Made from pure ivory, it glowed with a soft, pearly light. The throne was decorated with golden script, flowing like liquid, forming patterns and texts that represented knowledge, music, and art. The armrests were shaped like swans with wings spread in a protective gesture, symbolizing her role as a guardian of wisdom. At the top of the throne, a delicate veena was carved, its strings subtly vibrating as if an eternal melody played. The cushion, deep indigo and embroidered with symbols of creativity and intellect, invited all who approached to seek enlightenment.

Lord Indra's throne was a powerful symbol of his authority as the king of the gods. Made from storm clouds and lightning, it crackled with energy, humming faintly through the hall. Its surface displayed a dramatic scene of dark, swirling skies, with flashes of lightning lighting up the clouds. The armrests were shaped like thunderbolts, ready to strike at any moment. At the top, a crown of glowing jewels shone with an inner fire, symbolizing Indra's rule over the heavens. The seat, cushioned with soft clouds, was strong enough to support divine power. Sitting on this throne, Indra commanded both respect and awe, a true embodiment of celestial might.

Sage Agastya's throne was a symbol of ancient wisdom and simplicity. Carved from a single piece of sandalwood, it filled the celestial halls with a calming fragrance. The throne was decorated with detailed carvings of sacred texts, telling stories of creation, balance, and spiritual enlightenment. The backrest featured an engraving of a lotus in full bloom, symbolizing purity and cosmic knowledge. The armrests were shaped like meditative serpents, representing Agastya's mastery over kundalini energy and his deep connection to both physical and spiritual realms. The seat was covered with a simple saffron cushion, reflecting Agastya's ascetic lifestyle and pursuit of truth. This throne was a place of wisdom, inviting seekers to explore the mysteries of the universe and the soul.

The celestial halls of Mount Mandara were not just a meeting place, but a sacred space where divine will was carried out and cosmic balance was preserved. It was here that Vasuki, the powerful serpent deity, came to seek counsel, surrounded by the serene beauty and solemnity of this sacred setting.

Vasuki coiled gracefully at the center of the grand chamber, his emerald and gold scales shimmering under the celestial light. His eyes, deep as the space between stars, scanned the gathered assembly with a mix of determination and reflection.

Seated on thrones of light, the divine mentors observed him with expressions of curiosity and concern. These ancient beings embodied both creation and destruction, order and chaos. Among them were the wise Sage Agastya, with a beard like rivers of starlight, and the compassionate Goddess Saraswati, her eyes as calm and deep as the ocean of knowledge.

Agastya: (voice resonating with the weight of ages) "Vasuki, what brings you to this council? Your presence here is always a herald of great significance."

Vasuki uncoiled slightly, his form towering yet approachable. He dipped his head in respect before speaking, his voice carrying the echo of ancient mountains.

Vasuki: "Esteemed elders, I seek your counsel. The mortal realm beckons me, and I wish to walk among them, to understand their lives, their emotions, and their struggles."

A murmur rippled through the assembly. Saraswati leaned forward, her gaze piercing yet gentle.

Saraswati: (with a voice like a calming stream) "Vasuki, you have observed mortals for eons. What drives this sudden desire to abandon the comforts of immortality for the frailties of human existence?"

Vasuki: (pausing thoughtfully) "I have watched them, yes. But observation from afar is but a shadow of true experience.

Their joys, their sorrows, their love, and hate—these are mysteries I cannot fully grasp without living among them. I seek understanding, not from the divine vantage but through mortal eyes."

From his throne, the formidable Lord Indra, king of the gods, frowned, his brows knitting together like storm clouds.

Indra: "Mortality is a burden, Vasuki. Their lives are ephemeral, marked by suffering and uncertainty. You risk much by choosing this path."

Vasuki's gaze remained steady, unwavering.

Vasuki: "It is precisely because their lives are fleeting that they hold such beauty. Mortals find meaning in their struggles and purpose in their fleeting moments. I wish to comprehend this, to find wisdom in their brevity."

Saraswati exchanged a glance with Agastya, the two sharing a silent understanding. The sage spoke again, his tone a blend of caution and encouragement.

Agastya: "The path you seek is fraught with trials. Mortality will strip you of your divine powers, your memories will fade, and you will be vulnerable to the whims of fate. Are you prepared for such a transformation?"

Vasuki's form shimmered as he shifted, a reflection of his inner conflict and resolve.

Vasuki: "I am. To truly understand, one must immerse fully. I accept the trials, the pain, and the uncertainty. It is a price I am willing to pay for the knowledge and empathy that can only come from lived experience."

Saraswati: (nodding slowly) "Very well, Vasuki. Your journey will be a testament to your dedication. Remember, even in mortal form, the essence of your divinity will guide you. Seek the wisdom in their hearts and the truth in their eyes."

The council fell silent, the weight of Vasuki's decision filling the room. As the session ended, Vasuki felt a deep shift within himself, a mix of divine purpose and mortal curiosity. The path ahead was uncertain, but his resolve was strong. He bowed deeply to the council, his scales glinting in the light before he stood upright.

Vasuki: "Thank you, honored ones. I shall carry your guidance with me. May the heavens watch over my steps as I embrace the mortal realm."

The celestial hall fell silent as Vasuki turned to face the thrones, feeling the divine gaze upon him—full of concern, curiosity, and respect. Taking a deep breath, he closed his eyes and called upon his divine will, focusing on his transformation.

A radiant light surrounded him, glowing with emerald and gold. His form began to change, scales turning into skin, divine essence merging with mortal flesh. The process was both painful and freeing—a rebirth into a new existence.

A soft, radiant light surrounded Vasuki, glowing in shades of emerald and gold. The light grew brighter as he began shedding his divine form. He closed his eyes, focusing on the image of the mortal man he wanted to become—a seeker of truth.

The first feeling was intense heat, as though his very essence was being reshaped. His scales dissolved into a fine, iridescent dust that swirled around him and faded into the air. His long serpent body shrank and reshaped into a human form. His forked tongue fused into a single human tongue, and his slit pupils became deep, expressive human eyes.

Pain and freedom mixed as his divine essence merged with mortal flesh. His serpentine tail split into two strong, human legs. His arms formed from his coils, ending in human hands, once scaled and clawed, now nimble and ready to explore the world. The transformation was both painful and exhilarating, a rebirth that would give him the perspective he longed for.

As the light faded, his new form emerged—a man in his early forties with a lean frame, suggesting a life of intellectual pursuit rather than physical labor. His skin was warm and human, marked with the subtle imperfections of mortality. Dark, expressive eyes peeked out from behind wire-rimmed glasses framed by a square jawline and a neatly trimmed beard that gave him a scholarly air. His black hair was slightly tousled, adding to his thoughtful appearance.

Vasuki opened his eyes, now hiding his divine wisdom behind the gaze of a dedicated scholar. He felt the weight of his new life—the vulnerability and the incredible potential of living as a human. There was an exciting sense of freedom in his mortal form, a chance to fully experience the world's mysteries.

As he took his first step as a human, the celestial hall seemed to hum with approval. The divine had granted his wish, and with his new identity, he was ready to embrace the mortal world and all its experiences.

Agastya, who had been watching with a mixture of awe and respect, approached the newly transformed deity. Placing a reassuring hand on Vasuki's shoulder, he said, "Welcome to your new life. May your journey be filled with the knowledge and experiences you seek."

Vasuki nodded, a grateful smile playing on his lips. "Thank you, my friend. I will make the most of this opportunity."

With a final glance at the celestial thrones—now distant reminders of his divine past—he turned and began his descent from Mount Mandara. Vasuki, now Vikram, stepped into a world of mortal wonders and challenges, ready to embrace the life he had chosen.

The transformation from Vasuki to Vikram Nair had been profound and disorienting. As he descended from the celestial halls, the divine light gradually faded, replaced by the earthy hues and sounds of the mortal world. Vikram found himself standing on the outskirts of a small village nestled in the foothills of the Himalayas. The air was crisp and filled with the scent of pine and blooming wildflowers.

For a moment, Vikram stood still, taking in the world through human senses. The feel of the cool breeze against his skin, the sound of distant laughter and chatter, the sight of verdant hills rolling into the horizon—it was overwhelming in its vividness. He closed his eyes and took a deep breath, feeling the weight and presence of his new mortal body.

The transformation from celestial deity to mortal man had left Vasuki disoriented. The once vibrant memories of celestial halls and divine beings began to fade, replaced by the immediate reality of the earthly realm. His first steps brought him to an ancient forest, a place where the canopy was thick, and the air was filled with the scent of damp earth and the whispers of spirits.

He wandered deeper into the forest, feeling the life around him. The spirits of the trees, invisible to mortal eyes, whispered in an ancient language. Their words spoke of a time long past when magic filled the world. Though their voices were out of reach, Vikram could sense their presence, like fragments of a forgotten dream.

One evening, as the sun set, Vikram found a clearing bathed in soft light. In the center stood an old sage, his long white beard flowing like a river of wisdom. The sage looked up, his eyes gleaming with ancient knowledge.

Sage: "Welcome, traveler," the sage greeted. "I have been expecting you."

Vikram, weary from his journey, bowed respectfully. "Who are you, wise one?"

Sage Parashara: "I am Rishi Parashara," the sage replied. "And you, Vasuki, have chosen a path that few dare to tread."

Vikram's eyes widened in surprise. "You know my true name?"

Rishi Parashara nodded. "The forest whispers many secrets. Come, sit with me, and let us talk."

As they sat together, the sage spoke of the trials and tribulations that awaited Vikram. He spoke of the balance between the mortal and divine realms and the importance of maintaining harmony.

Rishi Parashara: "You have chosen to experience humanity, but remember, with great power comes great responsibility. The challenges you face will shape your destiny."

Vikram listened intently, the sage's words resonating deep within him. As night fell, the forest seemed to hum with a soothing melody, a promise of protection and guidance on his journey.

Leaving the ancient forest behind, Vikram found himself in a vast, barren desert. The sun beat down mercilessly, and the sand seemed to stretch endlessly in every direction. The harsh conditions tested his physical endurance, but it was the solitude that weighed heaviest on his heart.

Days turned into weeks as he wandered through the desert, his lips parched and his skin blistered by the sun. Yet, even in this desolation, he found moments of beauty. The shifting sands created patterns that seemed to dance in the wind, and the night sky, free from the haze of civilization, was a canvas of countless stars.

One evening, as he struggled to find shelter from a brewing sandstorm, Vikram stumbled upon a small oasis. There, he met a young nomad named Aarav, who offered him water and shelter.

Aarav: "You're not from these parts," Aarav observed, his eyes scanning Vikram's attire.

Vikram: "No, I am a traveler seeking understanding."

Aarav smiled; his expression was both kind and curious. "Then you have come to the right place. The desert has a way of revealing truths that the busy world often hides."

Over the next few days, Aarav and Vikram shared stories of their journeys. Aarav spoke of the nomadic life—the hardships and the freedom—and the deep connection to the land and stars. Vikram, in turn, shared tales from ancient texts, the myths and legends that had shaped civilizations.

As the sandstorm cleared, Vikram felt a renewed sense of purpose. The desert had stripped away his illusions, revealing his true self. With Aarav's guidance, he continued his journey, now more aware of his inner strength. From the barren desert, Vikram's path took him to a lively city, its noise and energy a sharp contrast to the peaceful desert and forest. People rushed about, unaware of the world around them.

Vikram found peace in the city's libraries and museums, where he immersed himself in books and artifacts that reflected humanity's search for knowledge. It was in one such museum that he met Dr. Maya Singh, a historian passionate about ancient mythologies.

Maya was immediately drawn to Vikram's insights and depth of knowledge.

Maya: "You speak of these myths as if you were there," she remarked one day, her eyes narrowing in curiosity.

Vikram: (chuckling softly) "Sometimes it feels that way. The past has a way of speaking to us if we are willing to listen."

Their shared passion for history and mythology quickly turned into a deep friendship. Maya's enthusiasm and inquisitive nature were a perfect counterbalance to Vikram's quiet wisdom. Together, they explored the city's hidden corners, uncovering stories long forgotten.

One evening, as they walked along the river that cut through the city, Maya turned to Vikram.

Maya: "There is something different about you, Vikram. Something … timeless."

Vikram: (pausing, considering her words) "Perhaps it is because I have seen the world through many lenses. Each experience, each place, leaves its mark."

Maya: (smiling, her eyes reflecting the city's lights) "I'm glad our paths crossed. There is much we can learn from each other."

Each encounter and emotion revealed the essence of humanity. Vasuki's journey was a collection of experiences that led to a deeper understanding of life. He realized that humanity was defined not by divinity, but by the strength to endure, love, and hope.

After years of wandering and learning, Vasuki heard whispers about a place called Chandravati. It was said to be a city of ancient wisdom, where the divine and mortal worlds met. The name resonated deeply within him, as though the city itself was calling to him.

One evening, as the sun set over the river, a warm golden light covered the water. Vasuki sat by the riverbank, deep in thought about his journey. The sound of the flowing water was calming, and the cool breeze carried the scent of distant forests. As he looked at the horizon, a figure approached—a traveling merchant, his clothes dusty and a satchel over his shoulder. The merchant's eyes sparkled with stories of many places, and his smile was friendly.

Merchant: "Good evening, traveler," the merchant greeted, settling down beside Vasuki. "May I join you?"

Vasuki: "Of course," he replied, curious about the stranger.

The merchant pulled out a small flask and offered it to Vasuki.

Merchant: "A sip of water from the mountains. It's refreshing after a long day."

Vasuki accepted the flask with a nod of gratitude. As he drank, he observed the merchant's weathered face, marked by the journey of many miles. There was a wisdom in his eyes, a depth that hinted at countless stories.

Merchant: "What brings you to this riverbank?" his voice gentle and probing.

Vasuki: "I seek understanding," he said, choosing his words carefully. "I've traveled through forests and deserts, cities and ruins. I've experienced much, yet there is more I need to learn."

Merchant: (nodding knowingly) "The quest for knowledge is a noble one. I've met many like you on my travels—seekers, wanderers, those driven by a thirst for the unknown."

Vasuki leaned forward, his curiosity piqued.

Vasuki: "Where should I go now?"

The merchant's eyes widened slightly, and he chuckled softly.

Merchant: "Ah, Chandravati is the place. It is a name that carries weight: a city of legends. Few have found it, but those who do are forever changed."

Vasuki: "Tell me more," he urged, eager for any information that could guide him.

The merchant took a deep breath, his expression becoming more serious.

Merchant: "Chandravati is said to be an ancient city, hidden from the eyes of the unworthy. It was once a place of great wisdom, where the divine and mortal worlds intersected. The ruins are said to hold secrets from the dawn of time, guarded by spirits and sages."

Vasuki felt a shiver run down his spine.

Vasuki: "How does one find Chandravati?"

Merchant: "It is not an easy path. The city reveals itself only to those who are destined to find it. Some say you must follow the signs—the ancient ruins that emerge from the earth, the mystical energies that fill the air. Others speak of visions and dreams guiding the way."

Vasuki nodded slowly, absorbing the merchant's words.

Vasuki: "And you, have you been there?"

Merchant: "No, but I have met those who claim to have seen its gates. Their stories are filled with wonder and mystery. They speak of Chandravati as a place where time stands still, where the past and future converge."

Vasuki's heart quickened with anticipation.

Vasuki: "Thank you, friend. Your words have given me hope."

Merchant: "May your journey be guided by wisdom and light. Remember, the true path to Chandravati lies not just in the physical journey but in the journey of the soul."

As the merchant stood to leave, Vasuki felt a deep sense of gratitude.

Vasuki: "Safe travels to you."

Merchant: "And to you," he replied, his eyes twinkling with a knowing light. "May you find what you seek."

Vasuki watched the merchant disappear into the dusk, his figure fading away. The river continued to flow, its soft murmur reminding him of time passing. With renewed determination, Vasuki stood up and prepared for the next part of his journey. The path to Chandravati lay ahead, and he was ready for whatever challenges it might bring.

In the quiet of a secluded forest, Vikram felt a strong urge to leave behind his divine nature and fully embrace his new human life. The change was slow but significant. As the divine fog lifted, he struggled to remember his celestial past. The memories of his life as Vasuki began to fade, replaced by a growing desire to understand and explore the mortal world.

In a dimly lit study, Vikram Nair sat at a cluttered desk filled with ancient texts, maps, and notes. The name 'Chandravati' had become a constant thought, a link to something greater. It felt like a whisper of destiny, leading him toward a new purpose.

He dove into researching Chandravati with intense curiosity, his pursuit becoming an obsession. Driven by a deep need to uncover the city's mysteries, he was drawn into the world of archaeology. His forgotten divine identity was replaced by the dreams and aspirations of a dedicated archaeologist.

Vikram's path into archaeology was filled with hard work and dedication. He enrolled in top institutions, earning degrees in history and archaeology. His studies focused on ancient civilizations, artifacts, and the mysterious history of Chandravati. His professors admired his commitment and passion, though they didn't know the deeper motivation behind his drive.

Vikram's colleagues and mentors often discussed his research with him. As he advanced in his studies, the memories of his divine past faded into dreams—brief and unclear. His attention stayed on his academic work, fueled by a strong desire to uncover the secrets of Chandravati and contribute to archaeology.

Vikram spent years searching through ancient texts and following mysterious clues to find the lost city of Chandravati. His journey started with a mention of the city in an old manuscript he found at Oxford. The manuscript described a city where the divine and mortal worlds met, hidden and protected by nature. Curious, Vikram spent endless hours studying maps and inscriptions that led him to Rajasthan.

After months of careful research and cross-referencing historical records, Vikram finally identified the likely location of Chandravati. He knew this discovery could change the understanding of ancient Indian civilizations, and his excitement was clear.

Next, he secured funding and assembled a team. Vikram reached out to trusted colleagues—Dr. Anjali Kapoor, Raj

Mehta, Maya Singh, and Rohan Patel—each bringing vital expertise to the project. With a university grant and a few private donations, they were ready to begin.

When they reached the remote village near the site, Vikram knew gaining the locals' trust would be difficult. The area was sacred to them, and their culture was filled with stories of divine protection and ancient curses.

Upon arrival, Vikram and his team were met with a mix of curiosity and suspicion. The village elder, Bhairav Singh, a wise and respected man, agreed to meet them to discuss their plans. The meeting was held in the village square, under the shade of a large banyan tree, with the villagers watching, their faces showing both skepticism and interest.

Vikram: "Namaste, Bhairav ji," Vikram began respectfully, bowing slightly. "We are honored to be here in your village. My name is Dr. Vikram Nair, and these are my colleagues. We have come to learn more about the history of this land and the stories it holds."

Bhairav Singh: (studying Vikram carefully) "What do you seek in Chandravati, Dr. Nair?"

Vikram took a deep breath.

Vikram: "We believe that Chandravati holds a significant place in our history. By uncovering its secrets, we can better understand our heritage and share it with the world. We come with respect and a desire to preserve, not to disturb."

Bhairav Singh nodded slowly, considering Vikram's words.

Bhairav Singh: "Our ancestors speak of Chandravati as a place of great power and divine presence. Many fear disturbing it. How can we trust that your intentions are pure?"

Dr. Anjali Kapoor: (stepping forward) "Bhairav ji, we understand your concerns. Our work is guided by principles of respect and preservation. We will ensure that the site is protected and that any findings are shared with the community. We wish to honor your ancestors by bringing their stories to light."

Raj Mehta: "Moreover, we believe that the knowledge we uncover could benefit the village as well. With greater understanding and recognition, there could be opportunities for education and development."

The villagers murmured among themselves, some nodding in agreement while others remained skeptical. Bhairav Singh raised his hand for silence.

Bhairav Singh: "We will allow you to proceed but under one condition. You must involve our people in your work and respect our customs and beliefs."

Vikram: (smiling, relieved) "Thank you, Bhairav ji. We promise to honor your condition and work together in harmony."

With the villagers' cautious approval, Vikram and his team began their work. They set up a base camp near the site, with tents and equipment organized. Local laborers, guided by Raj and Rohan, started clearing surface debris. Vikram and Anjali mapped out a grid for systematic excavation, while Maya documented the initial findings and Rohan set up equipment to scan for subsurface anomalies.

The first few days were slow, with careful digging revealing fragments of pottery and stone carvings. Each artifact was carefully cataloged and photographed, with Maya and Raj working to interpret what they uncovered.

As the days passed, the team's excitement grew. They discovered the foundations of what seemed to be an ancient temple, its walls covered in intricate carvings and symbols. The villagers, now more involved and curious, began sharing their oral histories and legends, offering valuable context to the findings.

One evening, Vikram stood at the center of the site, watching the sunset over the ruins. He felt a deep connection to Chandravati, sensing they were on the verge of something extraordinary. With the support of his team and the villagers, he knew they were ready to uncover the hidden stories of this ancient city.

Chapter 3: The Secret Society

Beneath the busy streets of Vienna, hidden from the modern world, lies the secret chamber of the Order of the Ecliptic. The name 'Ecliptic' reflects the society's role as a protector of balance, similar to how the ecliptic plane keeps celestial bodies in harmony. The founders believed that, just as the sun and moon follow the ecliptic, their society would navigate both the visible and invisible worlds to maintain order and prevent chaos.

This secret chamber, hidden in shadows, can only be reached through a series of complex passageways in the city's ancient catacombs. To enter, one must navigate a winding maze of tunnels decorated with mysterious symbols and faded murals of celestial battles and ancient rituals. Known only to a few, this underground network highlights the Order of the Ecliptic's deep secrecy and careful planning.

As one neared the hidden chamber, the air became cooler and quieter, the sounds of the city above fading away. The entrance was guarded by two imposing stone statues, each representing a celestial guardian, their eyes seeming to watch with eternal vigilance. Beyond these statues stood a large, intricately carved wooden door, reinforced with iron bands and decorated with the Order's sigil—a sun partially eclipsed by the moon, encircled by a ring of stars.

Upon entering, the hidden chamber unfolded as a vast, awe-inspiring space. The ceiling arched high above, supported by columns carved to resemble ancient trees, their branches intertwining to form a canopy of stone leaves. Lanterns made of wrought iron and crystal hung from these branches, casting a soft, ethereal glow that bathed the chamber in light.

The walls were lined with shelves and alcoves, each filled with treasures from across the ages. Ancient manuscripts, their pages yellowed and fragile, rested alongside arcane artifacts and relics from long-lost civilizations. Every item held a story, a history carefully preserved by the Order. The shelves themselves were crafted from dark, polished wood, etched with protective runes and symbols designed to shield the chamber's contents from misuse.

At the center of the chamber stood a large, round table made of dark mahogany, its surface inlaid with a mosaic of precious stones that portrayed the celestial ecliptic. The intricate design featured constellations, planetary alignments, and other celestial phenomena, all carefully arranged to tell the story of the cosmos. Surrounding the table were high-backed chairs, each one distinct, crafted to reflect the status and origin of its occupant.

To the north of the chamber, a grand fireplace roared with a controlled, mesmerizing blue flame, providing warmth and an otherworldly light. Above the fireplace hung a tapestry depicting the founding of the Order, a scene of ancient sages and celestial beings coming together to form a pact that would endure through the ages.

At the farthest end of the room, a big arched stained glass window showed an eclipse. The light and shadow on the stone floor made bright patterns. The window was magically made to show the real phases of the moon, even though it was buried deep underground. It was both a sign and a tool for the Order's magical practices.

But the most important thing in the room was an old stone altar sitting on a raised platform at the front of the room. There were glyphs and sigils on this altar that gave off a faint glow and pulsed with power that seemed to come from the earth itself. The most sacred rituals of the Order were held here, connecting its members with forces beyond human understsanding..

There was a strong smell of sandalwood, myrrh, and frankincense incense in the room, mixed with the musty smell of old paper and stone. The air was holy and mysterious, and it felt like time had stopped there. You could feel the weight of hundreds of years in every breath.

As the important people of the Order slowly walked into the room, there was an uncanny feeling of power and anticipation. Elder Matthias Richter, who was in charge of keeping secrets, was already sitting at the head of the table. He was tall and skinny, and wore a dark suit that was perfectly tailored. His silver hair and sharp, penetrating eyes gave him an air of both knowledge and power. Matthias was the strongest person in the Order. He had been in charge for decades and was highly respected by his peers.

As each council member took a seat, the flickering torchlight cast long shadows over their faces, adding to the air of power and secret in the room. The members of the Order each brought something different to the group. Together, their different backgrounds and strong skills made them a powerful force in the magical world. The way the seats were set up in the hidden room was both practical and symbolic. It showed the Order of the Ecliptic members' positions and responsibilities.

Matthias Richter, Elder, was sitting at the head of the big round table. He was known as the Keeper of Secrets. His chair, which was slightly raised on a dais, was fancier than the others. It had elaborate carvings that showed that he was the leader. The chair's dark wood was buffed to a high shine, and the thick, dark velvet seat was both comfortable and stylish. Being in this central place made Matthias's role as the main decision-maker and the Order's strategy's anchor stand out.

To Matthias's right sat Lady Eleanor Blackwood, in her late fifties. With sharp, intelligent eyes behind wire-rimmed glasses and silver-streaked hair often tied back in a loose bun, she dressed simply yet elegantly. Eleanor's calm, methodical approach to decoding ancient symbols and manuscripts was crucial to the Order's research. Her expertise provided the intellectual foundation for many of the Order's decisions. Her chair, though not elevated, was distinguished by a classic design and a comfortable seat. Positioned near the Keeper, she had easy access to the scrolls and manuscripts, allowing her to engage with the information and contribute to discussions on their arcane significance.

Sitting across from Eleanor was Sir Alistair Donovan, who was in charge of information for the Order and was a very active and careful person. Alistair looked tough and in charge, and his hair was cut short and colored in salt and pepper. He was the perfect boss for the Order's field agents because he had been in spies and secret operations before. His no-nonsense attitude and strategic thinking made sure that the Order's tasks were safe and successful. A big part of his job was to plan and run the Order's secret operations and protection. Because he had been in the military, the chair he was sitting in was simpler, stronger, and useful. The stark difference between his simple seat and the more ornate ones of his coworkers showed how serious he was about running the Order. Alistair's place across from Eleanor made it easy for them to talk directly about the intelligence and strategy parts of their discussions.

There was a psychic living with the Order named Madame Celeste DuBois sitting next to Alistair on Matthias's left side. The soft, flowing fabrics on her chair matched how airy and mysterious she seemed. Celeste was in her late forties and had long red hair and green eyes that looked like they could connect her to other worlds. Her soft but strong voice and flowing, bright clothes made her seem even more mysterious. Celeste's seat was placed to balance the energy of the table, which let her talk about what she thought the item meant on a spiritual and supernatural level while staying calm and on task. Celeste's job was to protect the artifact with practices and give advice on supernatural things that happened. These tasks were very important for understanding and controlling the artifact's magical powers.

It was Contessa Isabella Rossi who sat across from Celeste at the table. Her chair was beautifully made, with a high back and fancy upholstery that matched her height and job as a political planner. Isabella was in her late forties and had a statuesque body and striking beauty. Her dark, wavy hair framed her face. Her stylish and classy clothes matched how intimidating she was. Because of her job, she could hear and affect conversations about the Order's bigger social and political plans. Her wide range of contacts and political knowledge made her an essential part of managing the Order's relationships with other countries.

Hans Müller, an expert in technology and transportation, was sitting next to Isabella. He was an intelligent and quiet man who worked hard. Even though it was useful, his chair had a sleek, modern look that fit with his job of bringing technology into the Order's work. Hans was thin and looked like he was thinking. He looked young because he had short blonde hair and clear blue eyes. Hans' job was to make sure that the Order kept ahead of its enemies by combining cutting-edge technology with old knowledge. Hans was ready to deal with any technical or logistical problems that came up during the meeting because he was sitting close to a small desk with high-tech tools. His knowledge of technology and management was very important for running the Order's business and keeping their edge.

Lastly, the chair next to Hans was taken by Dr. Naomi Sato, who is an expert for the Order in Eastern beliefs and martial arts. The simple but comfortable design of her seat matched her calm and focused attitude. Naomi was in her early forties and had a beautiful, muscular body. She was also very calm. Her long, black hair was usually pulled back in a simple ponytail, and she wore clothes that were both practical and stylish. Naomi was a powerful person in and out of the field because she knew a lot about Zen and was very good at martial arts. Naomi was ready to share her ideas about what the artifact meant from an Eastern philosophical point of view since she was in a place where she could see both the strategic and practical talks. Her knowledge of Eastern beliefs often gave her a fresh look at the Order's spiritual and strategic issues.

Rajan Mehta's seat at the round table stood out because it was modern in a room that felt very old. Even though no one was sitting in the chair, it looked sleek and modern, and it had the newest hologram technology. A holographic image of Rajan came to life in the dim light of the room, giving off a soft, ethereal glow. Even though he wasn't there physically, his presence felt just as real as everyone else's. The advanced holographic system perfectly caught his focused look and manner. The clarity of his face and the steadiness of his voice told a lot about his ties to the Order and how important he was to their work.

The way the seats were set up around the table made it easier for people to work together and follow the rules, so everyone in the Order could make a good contribution to the meeting. Because of how the room was set up and where each chair was placed, everyone knew how important their job was and the atmosphere was good for strategic and intellectual discussion.

The Order members were getting together for a very important meeting. The Keeper was at the head of the table. His sharp, penetrating gaze, which scanned the room with an air of authority, made people appreciate him right away.

Matthias: "In Shadows, We Illuminate," he intoned solemnly, his voice echoing through the chamber, deep and resonant.

The Order responded in unison, "In Secrets, We Protect."

Matthias: "Let's begin," he said, his voice echoing slightly in the grand chamber. "Recent events compel us to address a matter of considerable importance."

He looked towards the physically empty chair occupied by the holographic projection.

Rajan Mehta's holographic image flickered slightly as he spoke.

Rajan: "Vikram's progress is promising. He's nearing a breakthrough with the artifact. Chandravati, I believe, holds the key to unlocking its true power. However, we must tread carefully. The village's history is intertwined with powerful and ancient forces."

Eleanor: (joining in, her fingers steepled) "Our latest deciphering of the ancient scripts points to an unprecedented alignment of events. The texts indicate that the convergence we've long anticipated is nearing."

Alistair: (his demeanor steely and resolute) "We've intercepted communications suggesting that other factions are becoming aware of Vasuki's reincarnation. We must act swiftly to secure our position and protect our interests."

Celeste: (with her ethereal presence) "The omens are clear," she said softly. "The spiritual energies around Chandravati are fluctuating. This signifies a convergence of fates. We must ensure we are prepared for what is to come."

Isabella: (ever the strategist) "We need to leverage our connections. The political landscape is shifting, and we can use this to our advantage. Our allies must be briefed, and our influence must be exerted where it will have the most impact. And all this must be done immediately."

Hans: (seated next to Isabella, speaking with quiet intensity) "I've been working on integrating our surveillance systems with the latest AI algorithms. This will give us real-time updates and predictive capabilities that are unmatched. We will know about any movements or threats before they materialize."

Naomi: (calm and composed, adding her perspective) "Our preparations must also include physical readiness. The ancient prophecies mention trials that are both spiritual and physical. We must ensure our operatives are prepared for both."

The Keeper nodded, his gaze moving from one member to the next.

Matthias: "We are at a pivotal moment. Our actions in the coming days will determine the course of events. We must be vigilant and unified in our efforts. Rajan, continue to provide us with updates from Vikram's team. Eleanor Alistair, coordinate our research and intelligence efforts. Celeste, Isabella, Hans, Naomi—prepare for all contingencies. The Order has safeguarded humanity from the shadows for centuries, and we will not falter now."

Eleanor spoke again, her voice tinged with the weight of their mission.

Eleanor: "The ancient texts are proving more complex than we anticipated. Every symbol, every word, holds layers of meaning. We must be diligent in our interpretation to avoid any missteps."

Alistair's eyes narrowed slightly.

Alistair: "Our field agents are on high alert. I've already dispatched a team to Chandravati to gather more intelligence. We need to ensure that any potential threats are neutralized before they can act against us."

Celeste's voice took on a mystical quality as she added,

Celeste: "The rituals must be performed with utmost precision. Any deviation could have catastrophic consequences. I will oversee the preparations personally to ensure everything is in alignment."

Isabella leaned back in her chair, her fingers tapping lightly on the table.

Isabella: "Political alliances are fragile at the moment. We must use our influence to stabilize the key regions. Our contacts in government and industry will be crucial in this endeavor."

Hans's expression was one of intense focus.

Hans: "The integration of our systems is nearly complete. Once operational, we will have unparalleled access to information. This will be our greatest asset in predicting and countering any threats."

Naomi's serene demeanor remained unchanged as she spoke.

Naomi: "Our operatives are training rigorously. They are prepared for any physical confrontations that may arise. However, we must also focus on their spiritual and mental fortitude. The trials ahead will test every aspect of their being."

Rajan's holographic image flickered again as he added,

Rajan: "Vikram is close to uncovering something significant. His discoveries could tip the balance in our favor. I will continue to guide him while ensuring our interests remain protected."

The Keeper stood, signaling the end of the meeting.

Matthias: "We have our tasks. Let us proceed with diligence and determination. The Order has stood for centuries, and we will continue to stand as the guardians of the hidden truths."

Matthias: "In Shadows, We Illuminate."

Assembly: "In Secrets, We Protect," the assembly echoed.

It was clear to everyone that their goal was very important as they started to split up. Each of them knew how important their part was in what was happening. There was more to the Order of the Ecliptic than just a hidden society. It was the force that kept the world safe from the unknown. They would protect humanity from the shadows that wanted to devour it as long as they stayed alert.

Chapter 4: City of Contrasts

The sky over New York City in the evening was a patchwork of deep purples and fiery oranges, which stood out against the city's landscape, which was a shiny silver. The Metropolitan Museum of History stood as a silent guardian in the middle of the city's steady pace, with the noise of the sprawling suburbs always in the background. There were many tall buildings in New York City, but the museum stuck out like a palace. Modern glass and classical stone materials put together in a way that stood out against the cityscape. The front of the building had tall, narrow windows surrounded by fancy stonework that gave it a royal but modern look. There were big, shiny columns at the entrance, and on either side of the imposing brass doors were carvings that showed scenes from history. People were excited as they climbed the wide stairs that went up to the main entrance.

The museum was a place of quiet respect and safety where the past could be felt in every corner. When people walked in, they saw a huge atrium with walls that seemed to reach the sky. The main hall was filled with light and room, and the walls were lined with tall displays and cases that showed off treasures from different times. The floor was made of smooth, shiny marble that reflected the light from the fancy lighting above. The chandeliers give off a warm, inviting light that brings out the intricate architectural features in the ceiling.

There were different wings of the museum, each with a focus on a different time era or theme. Each wing was very well put together, with carefully chosen artifacts and displays set up to tell a story. Soft, ambient lighting made each exhibit easier to see and created a calm mood. The air was filled with the smell of incense and the musty, faint smell of old artifacts, which made the museum feel even more real.

It took Dr. Vikram Nair a deliberate step to move through the museum's halls. His dark eyes, which were hidden by wire-rimmed glasses, were fixed on the old artifact that was taking over his thoughts. As he walked past displays showing how grand Egypt and Mesopotamia used to be, his attention stayed on one thing. The exhibits, which showed mummies wrapped in fancy linens and cuneiform tablets that spoke of lost countries, faded into the background of his mind.

He could not take his mind off of the mysterious artifact that was starting to make him feel uneasy. With its mysterious markings and old-fashioned vibe, the finely carved artifact seemed to be filled with a power that was both captivating and unsettling. Every time he looked at its picture or the strange symbols written on the paper, it made him feel more confused and intrigued.

Vikram's soft footsteps echoed off of the smooth marble floors, standing out against the background noise of people talking and the odd clink of exhibit cases being moved. His thoughts were a swirling mess of academic interest and increasing worry. The artifact's power was starting to show up in his dreams, making him see lost places and forgotten secrets. For him, it was more than just a piece of history; he felt like it was the key to something much bigger and maybe even more dangerous.

When Vikram got close to his office, he slowed down. The huge oak door with the brass nameplate that said 'His Title' stood in front of him. Before going in, he stopped for a moment and took a big breath. When he opened the door and walked inside, the smell of old paper and shiny wood welcomed him.

Being in a quieter part of the museum, away from the busy public areas, Vikram's office was a haven for deep research. It was immaculately clean and had shelves full of books and artifacts. The office showed how hard he worked in school and how well he knew what good looks like. The room was large and bright, with high ceilings and big windows that let in natural light and gave the room a warm glow. It was in a corner of the museum's study wing. Heavy drapes hung over the windows. They were usually pulled back to let in light, but they could be shut when needed to keep the outside world out.

Along the walls were wooden bookcases that were carefully stacked with old texts, archaeological journals, and reference books. There was a huge selection on the shelves, from old books about Mesopotamian history to new books about how to dig up things today. Artifacts and curiosities, like small statues, ancient coins, and relics from different cultures, were carefully cataloged and put on show among the books.

In the middle of the room was a big wood desk with a deep shine on its top. There were a lot of different things on the desk, like open study papers with Vikram's neat handwriting on them, a few well-used notebooks, and a brass holder with pens and pencils in it. With its green glass shade, the desk lamp focused light on the papers and lit up the area around the desk in a soft circle. A magnifying glass, which is often used to look closely at old writings or artifacts, was next to the lamp. A deep brown leather executive chair was set up behind the desk, and a smaller set of cushioned chairs in the same dark leather were in front of it.

A big corkboard on one wall was covered with drawings, photos, and maps that were all connected to the research that was still going on. The different items were linked by different strings, making a complicated web of data that showed Vikram's continued research into the artifact.

There was a tall filing cabinet in the far corner of the room. Its drawers were neatly labeled and full of old papers and study notes. Adorned next to the cupboard was a big globe that Vikram had used to study in his younger years. It had worn-out lines from old maps on its surface.

There were small, personal touches all over the room, like framed photos of archaeological digs, trip souvenirs, and a small, well-kept plant in a pot on the windowsill. The plant added a bit of green to the otherwise serious mood.

The general mood in the office was one of intelligent calm and alert energy. It was a place for Vikram Nair to work on the difficult parts of his job, surrounded by things that reminded him of how much he loved digging. Still, the room had an air of seriousness on top of the weight of the artifact's mystery, a tension that mirrored Vikram's own inner battle.

Vikram sat down in his leather chair in the poorly lit office. The worn leather made a familiar sound in the otherwise quiet room. The artifact, a relic in the shape of a serpent covered in gems, was placed boldly on the desk. It was both mysterious and disturbing to be there. The artifact seemed to be filled with energy from another world. Its subtle moves were hard to notice but could not be denied. Vikram was greatly affected by it and felt a constant shadow of unease that he tried hard to hide.

As Vikram's team got together for their daily meeting, there was a soft hum of talk in the office. His trusted coworker, Dr. Anjali Kapoor, sat in the corner of the big mahogany desk. Her work clothes, which were very practical, stood out against the serious atmosphere. A bunch of old papers were spread out in front of her, and she was studying them very carefully with her dark eyes. As Anjali took notes and sometimes looked through an old reference book, her concentration was clear.

Raj sat in one of the smaller chairs. His dark eyes moved quickly between his coworkers and the artifact-related materials that were on the table in front of them. They showed a mix of interest and worry. Raj was writing down his thoughts and observations about the ongoing study in a personal notebook. Even though he seemed calm and collected on the outside, there was a hint of tension in his stance that showed how hard it was for him to deal with all the information he was processing.

Maya Singh was now sitting in a comfy couch next to the desk. She was very interested in a stack of mythological and historical books. Her thin fingers were tracing sections while she made notes in a notebook. Maya's face lit up with flashes of understanding, and her eyes sparkled with joy as she made connections between the artifact and stories from the past.

The expert with a lot of tech knowledge, Rohan Patel, stood near the corkboard that was full of research-related sketches, photos, and maps. He was busy figuring out what the data on his tablet meant by entering different numbers and comparing them to what was shown on a big screen on the wall. Rohan was happy as he tapped away at the tablet and changed the screen with a mix of efficiency and interest.

Vikram: (his voice steady but his eyes betraying a hint of concern) "We need to discuss the recent findings and their implications. This artifact is proving to be more than just a historical curiosity."

Anjali: "I've been poring over these Vedic fragments. They describe a serpent deity that might be linked to our artifact. It talks about a divine guardian of secrets—one that was worshipped for its knowledge and wisdom."

Vikram: "Yes, that fits with what we've seen. The serpent is a common motif across various cultures, symbolizing wisdom and protection. This serpent motif we're seeing—it's not unique to one culture. It's pervasive. The symbolism seems to transcend boundaries. Take, for instance, the Nagas in Hindu mythology."

Anjali: (looking up from the books and manuscripts she was going through) "The Nagas, yes. In Hindu lore, they are serpentine deities associated with water and fertility. They're guardians of hidden knowledge and ancient wisdom. This might align with what we're seeing here. The Nagas are also linked to the cosmic balance and the flow of energy."

Maya: (rifling through a book on comparative mythology) "It's not just limited to Hinduism. Serpents are prominent in other cultures, too. In Buddhism, for instance, they are seen as protectors of the Dharma. They appear in several important texts and are believed to have a hand in preserving sacred teachings. This artifact might bridge various cultural understandings of serpents. The common thread is their role in guarding and revealing wisdom."

Rohan: (tapping and entering the data on his tablet) "That's intriguing. The artifact could be connected to these roles. If the serpent was seen as a guardian of wisdom, then it might have specific properties or powers tied to its mythological origins."

Raj: (scrolling through digital notes) "In addition to that, the serpent's connection to transformation is critical. In various cultures, serpents shed their skin, symbolizing renewal and rebirth. This aspect might be crucial in understanding the artifact's purpose."

Vikram: (agreeing with Raj) "Precisely. The concept of transformation is central to many mythologies. It represents the cycle of life and the passage between different states of existence. The artifact might be a key to accessing or harnessing these transformative properties."

Rohan: "That's a good point. We need to consider how the physical properties of the artifact relate to its symbolic significance. If it indeed holds transformative power, its composition might reveal more about its intended use."

Vikram: "Exactly. Let's also consider the Vedic references. The Nagas are linked to the cosmic balance and are often portrayed in association with significant mythological events."

Anjali: (turning a page in her manuscript) "In the Vedas, there are mentions of rituals involving serpentine figures to invoke protection and wisdom. The Vedic texts also mention a serpent deity named Vasuki, who was involved in the churning of the ocean of milk, the Samundra Manthan. Vasuki played a pivotal role in obtaining Amrita, the nectar of immortality."

Maya: (excitedly) "The churning of the ocean, or 'Samudra Manthan,' is indeed a key mythological event that connects with the concept of accessing hidden or divine knowledge. It was during this event that the nectar of immortality, the 'Amrita,' was obtained. If our artifact is connected to this event, it might be a relic of significant power and knowledge."

Raj: "The Mahabharata also describes the Nagas in various contexts."

Rohan: (thoughtfully) "If Vasuki is indeed connected to this artifact, we should examine any historical accounts of similar artifacts. There might be parallels that can provide insights into its functionality and purpose."

Anjali: "The ritualistic aspects are also important. In Hindu rituals, serpents are often used to channel divine energy or to invoke protection. The artifact could have been used in ceremonies that were intended to harness or direct these energies."

Maya: "And the concept of energy channels is also present in other cultures. For instance, in Chinese mythology, dragons, which are similar to serpents, are seen as controllers of rain and weather. The artifact might have a broader connection to elemental forces."

Raj: "We should also explore any potential connections between the artifact and ancient rituals involving serpents. If it was part of a ceremonial practice, understanding the specific rituals could provide insight into its purpose."

Rohan: "I'll dig into the technological aspects. The material composition and any unusual properties might give us clues about its intended use and significance. Also, I've been monitoring the artifact's energy readings, and there are some unusual fluctuations. They don't align with any known artifacts from this period. It's as if there's an external influence."

Raj: (scribbling notes) "The fluctuations could be related to the artifact's symbolic importance. If it's tied to Vasuki and the churning of the ocean, it might be exerting a psychological influence as well as a physical one."

Maya: (shifting in her armchair) "The Samudra Manthan was a pivotal event in Hindu mythology. It involved both gods and demons, and the artifact might represent a nexus of these divine forces. The balance between creation and destruction, renewal and chaos, is central to its meaning."

Vikram: (leaning forward, trying to maintain composure) "That's exactly what I've been feeling—an imbalance. It's as though the artifact is resonating with something deep within me, casting a shadow that I can't fully grasp."

Anjali: (her gaze intensifying) "What do you mean by a shadow? Are you experiencing something specific, or is it more of a general unease?"

Vikram: (hesitating) "It's hard to describe. There are fleeting visions—ancient battles, cosmic upheavals, and serpents. It's almost as if the artifact is tapping into some ancient memory or consciousness."

Rohan: (frowning) "If the artifact is causing these visions, it might be interacting with your brain's neural pathways. We should consider running neuroimaging studies to see if there's any correlation between the artifact's presence and your experiences."

Maya: "Vikram, are you sure these experiences aren't a result of stress or fatigue? The pressures of our research could be affecting your perception."

Vikram: (struggling to stay calm) "I've considered that, but it feels different. The artifact seems to hold a presence of its own—something ancient and powerful."

Anjali: (nodding) "We should approach this systematically. Let's look into historical records of artifacts tied to the Samudra Manthan and see if there are similar accounts of their effects on individuals."

Raj: (interjecting) "I've come across some references in historical archives that might be relevant. They mention artifacts with divine associations and their impact on those who come into contact with them. I'll pull up those records for further examination."

Maya: "The serpent in Hindu mythology is not only a symbol of power but also of protection and transformation. Vasuki's role in the churning of the ocean was pivotal—he held Mount Mandara in place and contributed to the emergence of the nectar of immortality."

Vikram: (his gaze distant) "Yes, Vasuki played a crucial role. But what if this artifact is more than just a symbol? What if it's acting as a conduit to something much deeper?"

Anjali: "That's an intriguing hypothesis. If the artifact is a conduit, it might be channeling ancient energies or consciousness. We need to explore any connections between these energies and your experiences."

Rohan: "I'll focus on isolating the artifact's energy patterns. There might be a specific frequency or signal that's interacting with your brain. If we can identify it, we might be able to understand its effects better."

Raj, who had been observing Vikram closely, noticed the subtle changes in his behavior.

Raj: "Vikram, are you feeling alright? You seem ... distracted."

Vikram: (forcing a smile) "Just the weight of our discoveries, Raj. Nothing to worry about."

But Raj wasn't convinced. He knew Vikram too well. There was something more, something Vikram wasn't sharing. The shadow over his thoughts was growing darker.

Vikram: (sensing Rajan's observation but not addressing it) "We should also consider any mythological references to serpents and their impact on human consciousness. There might be ancient texts or legends that provide insights into how such artifacts influence those who come into contact with them."

Maya: "I'll dig deeper into the myths surrounding serpents. In Hindu tradition, serpents are often associated with both creation and destruction. They represent the cyclical nature of existence, which could explain the artifact's dual influence."

Anjali: "The artifact's inscriptions mention the churning of the ocean, which brought forth both divine and demonic entities. If the artifact is a remnant of this event, it might be interacting with forces beyond our understanding."

Rohan: "I'll prepare a comprehensive analysis of the artifact's energy emissions and compare them with historical records of similar artifacts. We need to understand if there's a pattern or specific influence."

While the team kept interacting, Vikram's inner battle stayed a quiet distraction. His thoughts and dreams were being blocked by the artifact's shade, which was getting stronger. He had glimpses of holy images that he couldn't explain, which made him feel even more alone. Even though he tried to stay calm, he felt like he was about to find out something important, but he couldn't quite get the full truth.

Vikram: (attempting to refocus the discussion) "Let's make sure we document every detail. The more information we have, the better we can understand the artifact's influence and its implications."

Anjali: (resolutely) "Agreed. We'll compile our findings and analyze them thoroughly. This artifact could hold the key to understanding not only its own significance but also its impact on those who encounter it."

Maya: "And I'll continue to research the myths and legends associated with serpents and cosmic events. There might be additional clues in the stories that have been passed down through generations."

Rohan: "I'll start running the additional scans and analyses. We should have preliminary results soon."

Just as the meeting was ending, Vikram felt a mix of satisfaction and worry. It was clear that the item had an effect on him, and those effects were getting stronger. He was sure that the item held the answers, and he was determined to find out what it held, even if it meant facing his own doubts and fears.

The team split up, with each person focused on their own work. Vikram went back to his desk, where the artifact would always remind him of the old forces at work. Because the artifact had such a big effect on his mind, the divine views he had were both scary and enlightening.

Vikram: (to himself, as he gazed at the artifact) "What is this artifact truly hiding? What is it trying to tell me?"

Vikram's contacts grew throughout the day and went beyond the walls of his office. With its grand halls and stately displays, the museum was a center of intellectual activity. Vikram talked to museum staff, told his assistant about the upcoming show, and had a conversation with preservationists about how to keep things in good shape. He was authoritative but friendly at the same time, which was something he did with studied ease.

Vikram stopped in the Egyptian hall to look at a sarcophagus that had just been fixed up. The complicated hieroglyphics told stories about pharaohs and gods, which were similar to themes from ancient times that were important to his study. The Egyptian sarcophagus was an amazing piece of old art. It was hand-carved with hieroglyphics and had colorful pictures of gods and pharaohs on it. It told a story about respect for the afterlife. The holy symbols were emphasized by golden inlays, and the sarcophagus's face was calm, representing the endless peace that the dead sought.

As Vikram looked at the carved lines, he felt a strange link between the beliefs of old Egyptians and the Hindu mythology he had been learning. Indian ideas about rebirth and the spiritual realms were strongly connected to the focus on the afterlife and respect for divine beings. This link between the two ancient societies seemed to whisper to him, bridging gaps in time and space and deepening his understanding of how important the artifact really was.

A young curator approached him, breaking his reverie.

Curator: "Dr. Nair, the sarcophagus turned out beautifully, didn't it?"

Vikram: "Yes, it's magnificent," Vikram replied, his mind still half-occupied with thoughts of the artifact and the celestial serpent.

Vikram went outside the museum to find peace in the flow of the city. He liked to hang out in local coffee shops, where he could work on his studies without anyone seeing. Vikram often had moments of clarity here, where the smell of freshly made coffee and the noise of people talking were present. During his trips to these cafes, he would have short conversations with friends and acquaintances, but he would stay away from their conversations during these times.

Vikram was very alone in his small apartment, which was decorated with framed historical maps and photos of his trips. In the peace and quiet of his own home, he faced how the item was changing his thoughts and dreams. The ancient relic was making him have vivid, scary visions, which he carefully wrote down in a leather-bound notebook. Each note was proof of how deeply the artifact affected his mind.

The soft light from his desk lamp lit up the room as the day turned to night, making shadows that looked like they were dancing on the walls. Vikram was sitting at his wooden desk with a pen ready in his hand and the notebook open in front of him. He wrote with a ferocity that showed how troubled he was inside. His mind was racing to catch the fleeting images that kept coming back to him while he slept.

"June 16," he wrote. "The visions are becoming more frequent and more vivid. Last night, I dreamt of a vast serpent coiled around a mountain, its scales shimmering with an ethereal light. It spoke to me in a language I did not understand, yet the meaning was clear—a warning, a prophecy perhaps. I feel a deep connection to this being as if I have known it for centuries."

He paused, the pen hovering over the page, as the memory of the dream sent a shiver down his spine. The serpent's eyes had been hauntingly familiar, filled with an ancient wisdom that seemed to pierce through time and space.

"The artifact," he continued, "seems to be the catalyst for these visions. I must understand its origin and its power. It is more than a mere relic; it is a key to something far greater, something that my mind cannot yet fully grasp."

Vikram put down the journal, leaned back in his chair, and looked up at the sky. He had a lot of thoughts and feelings going through his head, and the lines between reality and the supernatural got less clear every day. He had a strong sense of duty as if the item had picked him to find out its secrets and keep its power safe.

The city noise outside his window was a soft hum that reminded him of the world he was slowly leaving behind. His coworkers and friends didn't understand how much he was going through. They only saw the scholar's work on the surface, how hard he worked. But behind that exterior, Vikram was fighting forces he couldn't understand, forces that were trying to swallow him.

He got up and went to the window to see the lights of the city. New York City was full of extremes. The past and the present lived together in a delicate balance. Seeing himself here, at the point where history and myth meet, seemed right, he thought.

The item seemed to become stronger as he stood there thinking. It was a real force that pulsed with its own energy. Vikram was sure he had to keep researching and learn more about the secrets around him. The answers were out there, in the old books and lost stories that had interested him for so long.

He went back to his desk, picked up the book, and felt more determined than ever. There was a lot to do, and time was running out. The artifact had picked him out for a reason, and he wouldn't stop until he had found out what it was hiding and found the truth that was hidden in the shadows of history.

The team got back together in Vikram's office the next morning. The air was thick with excited people and the smell of strong coffee. Vikram sat down at his desk and looked at his team. There was no one else around, and everyone was ready to get to work.

"Let's pick up where we left off," Vikram began, his voice steady but his mind in turmoil. "Anjali, any new findings?"

Anjali adjusted her glasses and nodded. "I've found more references to the celestial serpent. It seems to be a protector but also a harbinger of great change."

Maya leaned forward, her eyes gleaming with excitement. "This ties in with the myth of Vasuki. In Hindu mythology, Vasuki was wrapped around Mount Mandara to help churn the ocean of milk, which brought forth the nectar of immortality."

Rohan, who had been silent, finally spoke up. "I've detected more anomalies in the artifact. There are bursts of energy that don't correspond to any known source. It's almost as if it's trying to communicate."

Vikram's grip tightened on his pencil. The artifact's influence was becoming harder to ignore. "We need to be cautious," he warned. "The artifact is powerful and unpredictable."

Raj observed Vikram, noting the tension in his voice and the shadows under his eyes. "Vikram, have you experienced anything unusual? You seem ... different."

Vikram hesitated, then shook his head. "Just the usual stress of our work, Raj. I'm fine."

Raj wasn't sure, though. He reminded himself to pay more attention to Vikram. The team worked all day, with each person sharing what they knew. By translating the texts, Maya giving mythological views, and Rohan looking at technology, it became easier to see what the artifact meant.

As the hours went by, Vikram's inner fight got worse. Like a dark cloud over his mind, the item was always with him. But he kept quiet because he wanted to keep his team from having to deal with the stress he was feeling.

Anjali looked up from her manuscripts, her eyes shining with discovery. "I think I've found something. This passage mentions a prophecy linked to the celestial serpent and an artifact of great power. It speaks of a balance between worlds."

Maya's eyes widened. "This is huge! In many myths, balance is crucial. In Hindu mythology, the concept of dharma, or cosmic order, is central. If the artifact is disrupting that balance, it could explain the anomalies we're seeing."

Rohan nodded, his brow furrowed in concentration. "The energy bursts from the artifact ... they could be manifestations of this imbalance. We need to figure out how to stabilize it."

Vikram's head throbbed with the weight of their discoveries. "We must proceed carefully. The artifact's power is vast, and its influence is spreading."

Raj, ever perceptive, watched Vikram closely. "Are you sure you're okay, Vikram? You seem ... off."

Vikram forced a smile. "I'm fine, Raj. Just focused on the task at hand."

But Raj wasn't fooled. He could see the strain in Vikram's eyes, the tension in his posture. Something was deeply wrong, and he was determined to find out what.

That evening, after the team had dispersed, Vikram remained in his office, staring at the artifact. His mind was a whirlwind of ancient prophecies, mythological symbols, and unexplainable visions.

He picked up his leather-bound journal and began to write, detailing the latest vision: a serpent coiled around a mountain, its eyes glowing with an otherworldly light. He felt a deep connection to the vision as if it were a part of his own soul.

As he wrote, a voice echoed in his mind, a whisper from the depths of time. "Vasuki," it called, "guardian of the balance, remember your duty."

Vikram's hand trembled, the pencil falling from his grasp. He stared at the journal, the words blurring before his eyes. "What is happening to me?" he whispered, his voice filled with anguish.

He looked up, and the office around him went away for a moment. There was no longer a line between truth and imagination in that brief moment. Vikram was suddenly taken to a world from another world. The picture was so clear that it felt more real than his own surroundings. He saw a very large ocean, a very tall mountain, and a very powerful serpent. The vision was both scary and amazing; it showed him a world he couldn't understand.

He found himself on the edge of a huge ocean that went on forever. The water went on forever, and its surface was a deep blue sparkling plain. A rich fabric of swirling purples and gold made the sky look like it was getting dark, which made the scene feel eerie. The waves crashed with a steady force, and their roar was a mysterious and powerful melody.

In the distance, a huge mountain rose dramatically from the water. It had peaks that cut through the sky. The mist on top of them looked like it was lit from above. On the mountain's slopes, there were many old, weathered ruins that were only partially covered by the lush plants that stuck to the rock face. The mountain was both beautiful and scary, like a watchtower that stood watch over the realm with endless alertness.

Vikram's eyes were drawn to the serpent as they moved lower. It was a very big and powerful creature, and the way its body curled and uncurled belied its size. The scales of the serpent sparkled with a strange light, a hypnotic show of iridescent colors that changed as the serpent moved. Its eyes, which were dark and knew everything, seemed to cut through time itself and locked on Vikram with such force that it sent chills down his spine.

The shape of the serpent was both majestic and scary, a mix of beauty and danger. It moved back and forth, sending waves of energy across the ocean and up the mountain sides. When the thing was around, there was a low, resonant hum that seemed to come from the very center of the realm.

It seemed like Vikram and the serpent had a deep relationship, as if their fates were linked. The deep wisdom of the creature's eyes spoke straight to his soul in a way that he could not speak. The vision was both a warning and a discovery. It showed him a world he didn't fully understand.

Vikram felt a terrible feeling of dread as the vision started to fade. The serpent's eyes were still fixed on him. The realm, the ocean, and the mountain all seemed to fade away into a misty haze, and Vikram was startled back to the real world of his office.

As soon as he opened his eyes, sweat ran down his face. He took short, sharp breaths. He used to feel so at ease and at home in this office, but now it felt far away and strange. He was scared after seeing the vision, which was a powerful reminder of the artifact's power and mystery. He stared at the relic's display case for a long time. The artifact's mysterious presence always made him feel both intrigued and uneasy.

It was more than just a dream; he caught a glimpse of something huge and deep, a world that seemed to both scare and amaze him. Vikram knew that he had to figure out what he had seen in order to figure out what the vision meant. But for now, he had to deal with the disturbing thought that there were forces at work that he couldn't understand or control.

He forced himself to pay attention by shaking his head. He had to keep his cool for the sake of his team and the work they were doing. But the artifact was becoming more powerful, and he thought he was losing himself in it.

The next morning, the team gathered again. Vikram, determined to hide his inner turmoil, greeted them with a forced smile.

"Good morning, everyone. Let's continue our work. We're on the verge of something monumental."

Anjali, sensing his tension, offered a reassuring smile. "We're with you, Vikram. We'll figure this out together."

Maya nodded. "Absolutely. The myths hold the key. We just need to keep digging."

Rohan, always practical, added, "And I'll keep analyzing the artifact. We need to understand its energy patterns if we're to control it."

Raj, however, remained skeptical. He watched Vikram closely, noting every subtle change in his behavior. "Are you sure you're okay, Vikram? You seem ... off."

Vikram met his gaze, his eyes betraying a flicker of fear. "Thank you, Raj. I'll let you know if there's anything."

But Raj wasn't satisfied. He could see the strain in Vikram's eyes, the tension in his posture. Something was deeply wrong, and he was determined to find out the truth.

Chapter 5: Allies and Adversaries

Early in the morning, the sun gave Vikram's office at the Metropolitan Museum of History a soft glow. Its golden light came in through the tall windows. The room inside was a mixture of old knowledge and new goals. There were stacks of books, manuscripts, and scattered artifacts that told stories of other times and places.

Before anyone else came into the office, Vikram sat at his big desk by himself. It was the center of this intellectual haven. He was wearing a well-tailored suit, but his tie was a little too loose, which showed how tense the air was. His sharp, searching eyes looked out over the city's familiar sights, but now they had the strange weight of an old promise in them. The mysterious artifact seemed to have a life of its own as it lay still on a silk cloth. Its presence was both scary and appealing. Vikram couldn't get rid of the feeling that it was watching him and waiting for him to figure out what it was up to.

There was only the faint sound of traffic outside and the buzzing of an old clock on the wall to fill the room. Vikram's office, which is usually a calm and peaceful place, seemed to be filled with an uneasy strain.

Vikram ran his fingers through his hair. He was feeling a lot of different emotions at the same time. It was impossible to ignore the artifact; its detailed carvings caught the light in a way that made the surface of it look alive. Even though it wasn't moving, it felt like it was alive, like an ancient intelligence was sleeping and waiting for the right time to share its secrets.

He leaned back in his chair, listening to the leather creak softly under him, and gave himself a rare chance to be open and honest. Being in his office by himself with the item gave him the chance to let down his guard and stop acting like a sure-of-himself scholar. It seemed like the weight of the artifact in front of him made his doubts and fears stronger, as they echoed through the empty room. Vikram had a lot of strange ideas going through his head. They were a mix of academic interest and emotional turmoil. He had studied for years and found many strange things, but this item was the most disturbing thing he had ever seen. It was irresistible, drawing him in with a whisper of stories and histories that had been lost.

He looked at the artifact in front of him. Its presence was both intimidating and mysterious. It was a piece of history from another world, and the complex carvings on its surface held secrets. Its smooth stone seemed to have a life of its own, just like Vikram's heart was going through a lot of trouble.

Vikram took a slow breath and stared at the artifact, his eyes moving over the intricate designs on its surface. Each pattern looked like it was meant to be there, like a language he hadn't figured out yet or a message from a long time ago that he needed to understand.

In his mind, questions kept coming up. What was this thing really made of? That thing seemed to be calling to him so badly. What stories did it hold? The visions it gave him were clear and scary, pushing him to the edge of what he could understand. Vikram felt a huge duty because he was taking care of this old piece. He was in charge of finding out what the artifact's secrets were, but he knew that the way ahead was full of danger. There was more to his research than just finding out about the secrets of the past. He was walking a fine line between fact and fiction, history and legend.

He felt very bad about the thought. He felt the weight of expectation, both from his coworkers and the museum, as well as from himself. To find the truth, he had to be careful and brave, which were skills he had developed through years of hard schoolwork. But this job was different and went beyond what he had ever done before.

At times like these, Vikram thought if he was really ready for what was to come. He was having vivid, intense visions every night, which made him wonder where the lines between truth and dreams ended. They called to him like sirens, drawing him into a world of myth and magic that he had only read about in school.

A part of Vikram was excited about the task, even though he was scared. The past wasn't just a list of times and things; it was a living quilt made up of the lives of people who had lived before. The world is full of stories about ancient civilizations, their beliefs, and their struggles that are just ready to be found again.

Vikram realized how powerful the past was when he was alone. It was a force that could change the present and a source of knowledge that could help us understand the mysteries of being human. It was a link to the past and a key that could open doors he had never been brave enough to open.

Vikram felt a link to something bigger than himself as he looked at the artifact. He had a sense of purpose that went beyond his own fears. This was the reason he had chosen this road and spent his whole life studying history. It was a calling, a search to understand the events that had made the world what it is today.

Even though this goal gave him comfort, Vikram couldn't stop the storm that was building inside him. The clear and constant visions were unlike anything he had ever seen or felt before. Dreams weren't just that—they were windows into another world, one where time and space didn't make sense and where there were new, unknown things.

He could vividly remember the ocean, the mountain, and the serpent. Each one was like a collage of color and feeling. The ocean went on forever, and its depths held tales that had never been told. The rock stood guard, a reminder of how time can stand the test of time. The serpent, which was a majestic and powerful animal, moved with an ease that was both scary and beautiful.

These images were not just made up in someone's head. They told him what to do and made him question what he thought he knew about the world. They told him to look beyond what he could see and touch and into the worlds of myth and folklore that were just beyond the edge of what he knew.

Vikram knew he had to keep these dreams to himself, at least for now, even though they were very important. If he shared them with his team, it could cause doubt and throw off the careful balance of their work. He had to be the steady hand that held them up as they went through the rough waves of their research. But it wasn't easy to carry these lies around with you. Every day that went by, it got darker, like a cloud over his thoughts. It was always clear from the visions that the item had great power that should not be ignored or taken lightly.

Vikram wasn't sure if he was strong enough to handle this by himself. Being alone, which used to make him feel better, now made him feel like he was in jail, where his fears and doubts could grow because there was no light. Still, he knew that this silence was necessary because he knew that the time would come when he could tell people he trusted about these things.

The calm was broken when the office door opened. Maya Singh was the first person to walk in, and her presence filled the room with excitement. She was a bright historian who specialized in myths from the past. Her mind was as sharp as her fashion sense was varied. She wore a deep burgundy scarf today that added a splash of color to her otherwise stiff outfit.

"Morning, Vikram! I hope you haven't started the party without us," Maya said with a teasing smile, setting down her bag on a chair.

Rohan Patel followed a tech-savvy engineer whose fascination with the supernatural complemented his analytical skills. He was juggling a cup of coffee and a sleek tablet, his fingers tapping away even as he walked. "I've got some interesting data to share," he announced, his eyes gleaming with excitement. He was accompanied by Anjali Kapoor, who nodded at Vikram—a silent acknowledgment of their shared mission.

Raj Mehta finally joined the group. The rest of the team didn't know it, but he was a member of the secret Order of the Ecliptic and a very good scholar who could read old writings. But today, he felt like he had a weight on his shoulders and was becoming more and more conflicted as he tried to balance his different interests.

As the team got comfortable, Vikram took a quick look at each of them. The mysterious pull of the artifact was still fresh in his thoughts. The talk in the morning was very important. He wanted his team to be able to see past the obvious and understand the deep meanings of their study. They were slowly revealing the secrets to him, and he needed their help to figure them out.

"Alright, team," Vikram began, trying to sound as composed as possible. "We've made some significant progress with the artifact, but there's much more to uncover. I believe we're on the brink of something big, something that ties our world to ancient myths in ways we've never imagined."

Maya leaned forward, her eyes bright with curiosity. "You mean the connection between the serpent imagery we found and the Hindu mythology of Vasuki? It's fascinating. Serpents have always been symbols of power and mystery. In Hindu myths, Vasuki is a divine serpent, isn't he?"

"Yes," Vikram nodded. "Vasuki is one of the prominent nagas in Hindu mythology. He's often depicted as being wrapped around Lord Shiva's neck, representing strength and loyalty. There's also the story of the Churning of the Ocean, where Vasuki plays a crucial role as the rope used by the gods and demons to churn the ocean and retrieve the nectar of immortality."

Rohan looked up from his tablet, intrigued. "That's interesting, especially when you think about the artifact's energy signature. I've run some tests, and there's definitely something ... otherworldly about it. It's almost like it's alive."

Anjali, who had been leafing through a collection of ancient manuscripts, added her perspective. "The texts I've been translating mention a powerful serpent associated with a prophecy. It speaks of a time when the mortal and divine realms would collide, and only those with the wisdom of the ancients could restore balance."

As his colleagues shared their insights, Vikram felt a pang of guilt. He had not revealed the full extent of his experiences with the artifact. The dreams, the visions, the strange sense of familiarity he felt whenever he touched it. How could he explain the whispers in his mind, the feeling that he was on the verge of remembering something monumental?

He took a deep breath, steadying himself. "There's more to this than meets the eye. I believe the artifact is somehow linked to these prophecies and myths. But there's a part of me that feels ... connected to it on a deeper level."

The team paid close attention because they could feel how important Vikram's words were. Raj was paying close attention to him and noticing the small shake in his voice and the shadows under his eyes. Vikram had always impressed Raj with how hard he worked, but now he saw something else: a man fighting forces he couldn't control.

As the meeting went on, Raj could feel the weight of his own lies pressing down on him. The Order of the Ecliptic had asked him to keep an eye on Vikram's progress and report back to them on what they found about the item. But as he learned more, he became more worried about what the Order was really up to.

He looked at his coworkers and felt bad about himself because he didn't want them to know about his secret loyalty. They worked hard to find facts that could change the world because they were dedicated and passionate. He had to play both sides because he was stuck in a web of lies.

He felt torn inside because he was loyal to his friends but had to follow the Order's rules. It was time for him to make a decision about where his true loyalty lay. Raj made up his mind to pay close attention and find the truth that was buried under layers of old myths and current lies.

The office conversation got more lively as each team member added their own knowledge to help figure out what the item meant. Maya, who had always been skeptical but was now a believer, was busy putting together the mythological signs that seemed to fit with what they had found.

"You know," Maya mused, "there's a theory that many myths were actually based on real events. What if these stories of gods and serpents are echoes of a forgotten reality, a time when humans and divine beings coexisted?"

"That's precisely what I'm starting to believe," Vikram said, encouraged by her enthusiasm. "The myths might be more than just stories—they could be the key to understanding our past and shaping our future."

Rohan chimed in, his analytical mind racing with possibilities. “If that’s the case, then the artifact could be a remnant of that era, a conduit between worlds. What if it holds the power to unlock ancient knowledge?”

Anjali, always the voice of reason, tempered their excitement with caution. “But we must tread carefully. There are dangers in meddling with forces we don’t fully understand. Legends often warn of the consequences of such hubris.”

Vikram listened to his team and was grateful for their dedication and insight. Despite the inner turmoil that threatened to overwhelm him, he found strength in their resolve. Together, they were forging a path through the unknown, guided by a shared vision.

“I agree, Anjali. We must be vigilant,” Vikram said, his voice steady. “But I believe we’re on the right track. This artifact could change everything we know about history, about humanity’s place in the cosmos.”

It felt like everyone in the room had a goal and was determined to see their quest through to the end. But Vikram didn’t know what the future held. The artifact’s shadow was big and told him things he wasn’t ready to hear yet.

As the meeting came to an end, Vikram felt a stronger need to act quickly. He knew that the path ahead would be dangerous and full of problems that would test their faith and determination. But having his team by his side gave him hope. He thought that they could find the truth and save the world from the darkness that was trying to swallow it.

Late that night, after all of his coworkers had left the museum, Raj was in his office by himself. As he got ready for the imaginary meeting with the Order of the Ecliptic, the light from his laptop screen lit up his face.

Raj's office, which was hidden in a quiet part of the Metropolitan Museum of History, was a haven for smart and curious people. The soft glow of old brass lamps lit the room, illuminating the many artifacts and papers that were spread out around it. In the middle of the room, there was a big desk covered in Post-it notes with hastily written ideas and vague warnings on them. These notes showed that Raj's mind was always full of thoughts. Along with modern electronics, there were old manuscripts, some written in Sanskrit and others in scripts that have been lost. A bronze figure of Ganesha, the Hindu god of wisdom, stood proudly next to a sleek laptop. This showed that Raj was combining old knowledge with new technology.

The office also showed Raj's two selves. There were hints in his scholarly work about the secret work he did with the Order of the Ecliptic. His coworkers couldn't see the encrypted notes and messages that were kept in a locked box, but they gave them a look into the dark world he lived in.

This room wasn't just an office; it showed what kind of person Raj was—a place where serious work and secrets mixed and where the search for knowledge had no limits.

Before starting the private video call with the Order's council, he took a deep breath and steadied himself. Even though he had been to this meeting many times before, something about it felt different today. Today, he had the disturbing knowledge that his loyalty was being put to the test.

The screen came to life and showed the familiar faces of the council members of the Order. They looked like shadowy figures with dark features, which was done on purpose to keep their identities and power secret. Elder Matthias Richter, the mysterious boss of the Order, was sitting in the middle of the virtual table. Even though his speech was calm, it had a tone of authority that made you want to follow him.

"In Shadows, We Illuminate," the Keeper's voice was as commanding as ever.

"In Secrets, We Protect," Raj responded.

The Keeper's voice, authoritative and resonant, broke the silence. "Rajan Mehta," he began, using his full name with an air of solemnity, his words echoing with a weight of expectation. "We trust that your time with Dr. Nair has proven fruitful."

Raj nodded, clearing his throat to steady his voice. "Indeed, Keeper. Dr. Nair has made significant progress in understanding the artifact's inscriptions. His work has uncovered remarkable insights into the artifact. We've begun to see connections between the myths of ancient Hindu civilizations and the artifact's potential capabilities. The inscriptions are not merely decorative; they reveal a language that bridges ancient mythologies with potential scientific advancements. It's as if the artifact is a key to unlocking a forgotten era of innovation."

He paused, gauging the Order's reaction. The council members remained silent, their unreadable expressions urging him to continue.

He hesitated for a moment, then pressed on, his conviction fueling his words. "I believe this artifact has the potential to bridge ancient mythologies with modern science and technology. Imagine using its secrets to enrich our understanding of the past and innovate for the future. We could harness its power for the good of the world, revealing truths that could benefit humanity in ways we've never imagined. This is why I believe the artifact should be used to connect mythology with science and technology, bridging the ancient with the modern. It has unlimited possibilities—using its secrets to advance our understanding of both history and contemporary science. It could be a beacon for humanity, guiding us toward a future where the past and present coexist in harmony."

The silence that followed, stretching for what felt like an eternity, was deafening. Raj could feel the weight of the council's scrutiny, their collective judgment pressing down on him.

Finally, Madame Celeste DuBois, the Order's resident mystic, spoke up, her tone dismissive and cold. "Rajan, your enthusiasm is admirable. However, you must understand that the artifact's power is not to be squandered on utopian dreams. It is not a tool for public enlightenment. It is a weapon, a key to control and power that must remain under the Order's command. Its purpose is to fulfill the Order's ambitions, not to play into the idealistic fantasies of bridging past and present. It is a tool of control, one that the Order must wield with precision and purpose. Our purpose."

Her words struck Raj like a blow, each syllable eroding the hope he had carried into the meeting. He had anticipated resistance, but the outright rejection of using the artifact for a greater good was more disheartening than he had imagined.

Eleanor Blackwood, the English scholar of ancient languages and rituals, chimed in. "The artifact is meant to serve the Order's ambitions, Rajan. Its mysteries are ours to command, not to be shared with the world at large. Control over such power must remain absolute. The artifact's power is not to be underestimated or diluted by frivolous pursuits of altruism. We control history; we shape the future. That is our duty and our privilege."

Raj's heart raced, his frustration bubbling to the surface and conviction urging him to push back. "But this power doesn't belong to us alone! It's a legacy of humanity, a bridge between our past and our future. We have the opportunity to do something unprecedented—to learn, to teach, to unite. Just think about what this could mean for our understanding of human history! For decades, scholars have tried to piece together the mysteries of ancient civilizations. This artifact could be the bridge we've been searching for—a chance to connect the threads of our past with the possibilities of our future."

His voice was steady, but inside, he was a maelstrom of emotions. He knew he was challenging the very essence of what the Order stood for, but he had to make them see reason. There was a brief pause, and Raj dared to hope that his words might resonate with at least one member of the council.

"Imagine what could be achieved if we worked with the world instead of in the shadows. We could bridge the gap between science and mythology, using the artifact as a means to explore and expand our collective knowledge."

The Keeper's gaze was inscrutable, his voice cool and unyielding. "Rajan, your vision is indeed grand, but it is not the vision of the Order. The artifact must remain under our control, serving our directives. It is not your place to redefine its purpose." The Keeper's voice was firm, leaving no room for debate. "Your passion is commendable, but your priorities must align with the Order's. The artifact will serve its intended purpose, and that purpose is dictated by us, not by your idealistic aspirations. Remember where your loyalties lie."

Raj opened his mouth to argue, but Matthias cut him off with a wave of his hand.

"Remember your place, Rajan. The Order's interests must be safeguarded above all else. Your passion is commendable but misguided. We cannot allow sentimentality to cloud our judgment."

Raj swallowed hard as the Keeper's words hit him like a ton of bricks. The Order had made their position known, and no one could change it. The artifact was just a way for them to show that they were in charge of history and information.

Raj's heart sank as the truth of his position hit him like a cold wave. He had once thought that the Order was a group of wise people, but it wasn't. They kept power for themselves by changing history and using the artifact's power for their own gain. They would do anything to stay in charge. He used to think that the Order was a good group that kept secrets safe, but it turned out that they were more interested in power than in education.

He knew right then that his ideals were no longer the same as theirs. They wanted to be in charge, while he wanted to use the treasure for the greater good and see how it could bring about positive change. As he thought about Vikram and the team, the sincere conversations and shared desire to learn had stirred something real in his heart. They didn't see the artifact as a weapon, but as a sign of hope.

As the meeting continued, Blackwood's words echoed in his mind: "We control history; we shape the future. That is our duty and our privilege." His mind was elsewhere, mulling over the path he would now choose. Raj found himself withdrawing, his mind racing with thoughts of betrayal and duty. The weight of his decision pressed heavily on his shoulders. Could he truly turn his back on the Order, knowing the consequences?

But the answer was clear. He couldn't ignore his conscience, the belief that knowledge was meant to be shared, not hidden away for the benefit of a select few. The Order demanded loyalty, but his conscience called for something greater: integrity, truth, and the courage to break free from their chains.

As the meeting drew to a close, the Keeper delivered his final words, a veiled threat that lingered in the air. "Rajan, the Order expects your unwavering support. Betrayal is not an option you can afford to entertain. We expect your full cooperation. Remember, loyalty to the Order is paramount."

After those words, the screen went black, leaving Raj alone in his office's dim light. When he sat there in silence, his heart was full of fear and resolution. The choice he made weighed on him like a blanket. It was clear not only what the Order wanted but also what he had to do.

In the middle of the uncertainty, a new resolve began to grow. He was going to stand with Vikram and the team, with those who wanted to use the artifact's powers for the good of everyone—those who wanted information and understanding, not power.

The artifact was more than just a piece of history; it was a sign of the possibilities that existed where history, mythology, and current science met. It was important to Raj to protect that promise, even if it meant going against the Order he had sworn to serve.

Raj took a deep breath and got up from his chair. He was ready to face the difficulties ahead with his new friends by his side. There was no way to go back now that the path was clear. He would no longer be a tool for what the Order wanted.

Raj went back to the job at hand. He felt like he had crossed a line that he could never go back from. He now supported Vikram and his team, which was made up of dreamers and scholars with different backgrounds but with similar goals.

When Raj joined the team again, he seemed more determined than before. He went into the office with them and joined the lively conversation going on there. On the big oak table, there were both books and scrolls spread out all over it, as well as digital tablets showing detailed pictures of the item.

The item, which was both beautiful and scary, was sitting in front of Vikram, who was the leader and a scholar at ease. In the dim light, its complicated patterns looked like they were shimmering, creating strange shadows that moved around the room.

"Raj, you're just in time," Vikram called out, his voice drawing Raj from his contemplation. There was a warmth in Vikram's tone, a genuine eagerness that made the scholarly gathering feel more like a reunion of kindred spirits.

Raj settled into a leather chair that protested under his weight with a soft groan. "I'd love to hear more," he replied, his voice tinged with enthusiasm that surprised even himself.

Vikram leaned forward, his eyes alive with the glow of discovery.

"In Hindu mythology, the concept of cyclical time is prevalent—yugas, or epochs, that repeat over millennia. The artifact seems to allude to these cycles, suggesting that it could potentially interact with these temporal loops."

Raj paid close attention, his mind running with all the ideas they were making him think of. Myth and science came together in a way that was very interesting, like a fabric with threads from the past and the future. He could see how their ideas linked old stories to the present in new ways that he hadn't thought of.

Rohan stood by the window with his arms crossed and an uneasy look on his face as he watched the team. Rohan had always been the one to question the more general links that the others made. He was known for being practical and technically skilled. "Forgive me for my skepticism. I've seen the data, and while it's intriguing, it still seems a bit of a leap to tie it to grand mythological concepts. Can we truly say that these myths aren't just allegorical? What's the evidence linking this artifact to such grand concepts?"

Vikram smiled, understanding Rohan's reservations. "I completely understand, Rohan. Let's start with the basics." He pointed to a projection on the wall displaying a complex series of symbols from the artifact alongside graphs from Rohan's data. "Look here. The patterns in these inscriptions match astronomical cycles recorded by ancient civilizations.

Your data shows electromagnetic fluctuations that correspond with these cycles."

Rohan moved closer, his eyes narrowing as he examined the display. "Alright, I'll admit that's intriguing. But it could still be a coincidence."

Maya interjected, her voice filled with enthusiasm. Her eyes sparkled with curiosity, reflecting the artifact's enigmatic allure. "It's not just about patterns, Rohan. Think about the Samudra Manthan, the churning of the ocean in Hindu mythology. Vasuki, the serpent, was used as a rope by the gods and demons to churn the ocean and create amrita, the elixir of immortality. This story could be more than just a myth. The artifact might be a key to unlocking forgotten knowledge about these stories."

She pulled up a digital rendering of an ancient mural depicting the Samudra Manthan on her tablet. "This artifact has similar iconography. See the serpent-like engravings and the swirling patterns? They echo the cosmic themes from the myths."

Rohan nodded slowly, intrigued despite himself. "It's certainly a compelling visual parallel. But again, myths are allegorical. How do we know this isn't just symbolic?"

Anjali leaned forward, her glasses catching the light. "Myths often carry kernels of truth, Rohan. They're shaped by the cultures that bore them, yes, but they also serve as historical records. The artifact's inscriptions are a linguistic bridge between several ancient scripts. Some of the phrases we've translated suggest a narrative that aligns with cosmic events described in myths."

She tapped her pen against her notebook. "For instance, the term 'Kaalachakra' appears multiple times. It refers to the wheel of time—a concept that resonates deeply with Hindu cosmology and our findings about temporal cycles."

Rohan rubbed his chin thoughtfully, beginning to see the connections. "I see. If these inscriptions are more than decorative, they might indeed hold information we haven't fully grasped."

Raj looked up from his notes, his gaze meeting Rohan's. "Your own data, Rohan, shows something remarkable. The artifact emits frequencies that are eerily similar to those used in ancient Vedic rituals—specifically those aimed at achieving higher states of consciousness."

He pulled up a chart on his tablet, highlighting specific frequency patterns. "You can't deny the match. The ancient Vedas often spoke of sound as a powerful force—mantras and chants that could influence reality itself. This artifact might be designed to harness those very principles."

Rohan stared at the data, his resistance wavering. "I have to admit, those correlations are hard to ignore. But how can we prove this isn't all a fascinating coincidence?"

Vikram leaned back, allowing the conversation to unfold before jumping back in. "Rohan, think about how many scientific discoveries were initially inspired by myth or philosophical pondering. Mythology often provides a framework for understanding the universe in ways that science eventually catches up to. The alignment of our findings with these ancient stories might not be mere coincidence, but a revelation of forgotten knowledge."

He gestured to the artifact, its surface shimmering under the lamp's light. "This might be the bridge between ancient wisdom and modern science. Our task is to understand how these ancient concepts can be explained through the technology we have today."

Rohan uncrossed his arms and stepped closer to the table, looking intently at the artifact. "Alright, I'll bite. If there's even a chance that this thing is more than a historical curiosity, it could be groundbreaking. But how do we proceed from here?"

Maya grinned, sensing Rohan's growing curiosity. "We continue to decode the inscriptions and analyze the data. With your technological expertise, we can design experiments to test our theories. Imagine if we could recreate the conditions described in the myths and measure their effects with modern tools."

Anjali added, "We need to explore the artifact's origins further. Where it came from, how it was used, and why these patterns exist. It's a multidisciplinary approach, combining history, technology, and myth."

Rohan nodded, his earlier skepticism giving way to a sense of wonder and possibility. "You've got me interested. If there's a chance this artifact is as significant as you say, I want to be a part of unraveling its mysteries."

Vikram smiled, feeling a sense of camaraderie and shared purpose filling the room. "That's the spirit, Rohan. Together, we can unlock the secrets of this artifact and potentially redefine our understanding of history and science."

Raj was quietly happy as he watched the team continue to talk about their plans. He felt good about his choice to help

Vikram and the team, and he knew that working together could lead to finds that were far beyond what the Order of the Ecliptic could have imagined.

That moment, everyone in the group was working toward the same goal because they were all interested in the unknown and couldn't wait to find out more. The artifact, which had been a source of mystery and doubt, had changed into a sign of hope and unity, leading them on a trip that connected the old and the new. Myths and technology danced together in a complicated waltz of discovery, and its appearance showed how different times came together.

The artifact sat still in the middle of the table during the meeting. Its mysterious carvings seemed to be telling secrets from a long time ago. Its surface was a mosaic of complicated patterns and strange symbols. It had a soft energy that demanded attention and reverence.

Vikram regarded it with a mixture of awe and responsibility. "This piece of history," he said, gesturing towards the artifact, "is more than a relic of the past. It's a key—perhaps even a roadmap—to understanding how our ancestors perceived the universe and their place within it."

Maya nodded, her eyes reflecting the weight of his words. "And if we can decode its messages, we might uncover insights that have been lost for centuries—truths that could reshape our understanding of both history and the present."

Raj sat still and took in what was going on around him. The item was more than just a study tool; it was a metaphor for his own journey from doubt to clarity, from lying to telling the truth. The fact that he could touch it showed how much guts he had to stand up to the Order's dark goals and show his newfound loyalty to Vikram and the team.

He had a turning point when he recently met with the Order virtually. It was at that moment that the Order's good goals were shown to be lies. Instead of seeing the treasure as a way to bring people together and help them understand each other, the Order wanted to use its power for their own purposes.

Rohan, now fully engaged, leaned forward and studied the artifact with newfound curiosity. "If this really is a link between the ancient and the modern, how do we begin to unlock its potential? How can we test our theories without damaging something so precious?"

Anjali replied, her voice calm and reassuring. "It's about balance, Rohan. We must respect the artifact's integrity while employing modern techniques to explore its properties. This is where your expertise comes in—using technology to measure and interpret what we find."

She gestured to the array of equipment they had assembled: spectral analyzers, electromagnetic sensors, and 3D imaging devices. "With these tools, we can investigate without intrusion, allowing us to peer into the artifact's secrets while preserving its sanctity."

The room was alive with energy as the team set to work, their conversations a blend of excitement and purpose. Ideas flowed freely, and plans took shape, each step carefully measured and executed.

Chapter 6: The Prophecy Revealed

The grove felt like a refuge from another world, where the lines between them seemed to blur. It was lit up like the sun, and the air was filled with the sweet smell of divine plants and the soft sound of mysterious bells. Lord Shiva stood in the middle of it, giving off an aura of great peace and power. His presence was a mix of rough asceticism and the glory of God.

Vasuki, the primordial serpent deity, was curled up in front of him. His scales sparkled with a rainbow of celestial colors, reflecting the holy light that filled the grove. Even though he was huge and godly, there was a clear tension in his eyes, a rare glimpse of weakness.

While sitting on a beautiful mount, Lord Shiva slowly opened his third eye. The look inside it held all the knowledge in the universe. His rich, deep voice broke the peaceful silence.

Lord Shiva: "Vasuki, the time has come for you to prepare for the trials that await you. You have chosen to walk among mortals, to bear the weight of their world. This path is fraught with both peril and potential."

Vasuki, uncoiling to present himself with humility, spoke with a voice that seemed to echo the resonance of the universe itself.

Vasuki: "Great Lord, my journey among mortals has been enlightening yet fraught with complexities. The artifact I carry—its influence is profound, and its secrets remain elusive. I seek your guidance on how to wield its power for the greater good."

Lord Shiva tilted his head, his eyes reflecting the cosmic dance of creation and destruction.

Lord Shiva: "The artifact is a conduit between the mortal realm and the divine. It holds the power to alter the very fabric of reality, but its influence must be balanced with wisdom. You are to guide its use in a manner that preserves the cosmic equilibrium."

Vasuki: "And how shall I discern the path of balance? The artifact seems to interact with both the celestial and the mundane in ways I scarcely understand."

Lord Shiva: "The artifact's power is as ancient as the cosmos. It resonates with the cycles of time, the cosmic dance that governs the universe. You must attune yourself to these cycles, understanding the rhythms of creation and destruction."

Vasuki: "But the artifact also seems to evoke a deep resonance within mortals. Their fears and hopes, their aspirations—how do they intertwine with its power?"

Lord Shiva: "Mortals are vessels of both light and shadow. The artifact's influence can amplify their deepest desires and fears. Your role is to guide them, ensuring that the artifact's power serves to uplift rather than to bring chaos."

Vasuki: "I am concerned about the forces that seek to misuse the artifact. There are those who might exploit its power for their own ends, disrupting the balance you speak of."

Lord Shiva: "Indeed, there will be adversaries who covet the artifact's power for their own agendas. It is essential to identify true allies who share your vision of harmony. Trust in your intuition and the bonds you form with those who seek wisdom rather than dominion."

Vasuki: "How will I recognize these allies? And how can I ensure that the artifact's power is used responsibly?"

Lord Shiva: "Look for those who exhibit humility and a desire to understand rather than to control. Their actions will reflect their intentions. The artifact's power must be wielded with a spirit of unity and respect for the cosmic balance."

Vasuki: "And what of my own fears and doubts? Will they not cloud my judgment?"

Lord Shiva: "Fear and doubt are natural companions to great responsibility. Embrace them as part of your journey, but do not let them paralyze you. The path you walk is one of growth and discovery, both for you and for those you guide."

Vasuki: "Thank you, Lord Shiva. Your wisdom is a beacon in the darkness. I will endeavor to follow your guidance and protect the balance between realms."

Lord Shiva: "Remember, Vasuki, the balance between creation and destruction is delicate. Even in the face of adversity, strive to maintain harmony. The fate of the realms depends on the choices you make."

As Lord Shiva's body started to fade into the mists of heaven, his last words stayed with Vasuki like a heavenly blessing, giving her a new sense of purpose. The grove, which used to be a peaceful place, seemed to be pulsing with the stress of the job that lay ahead. With divine guidance imprinted on his mind, Vasuki was ready to start his journey as a mortal. He was ready to deal with the artifact's complicated power and the challenges that lay ahead of him.

The team gathered around their collection of study tools and old books, and the room was very busy. A lot of old manuscripts, mysterious artifacts, and high-tech tools made it possible for someone to work very hard on their thinking. Vikram, Maya, Anjali, Raj, and Rohan were working hard together to figure out what the item meant. There was a high level of stress and excitement in the air.

Vikram's gaze shifted from the artifact to the scattered papers. "We've made significant progress," he began, his voice steady despite the weight of the moment. "What we have discovered is more than just historical curiosity—it's a prophecy, and it's crucial we understand it fully."

Maya leaned forward, eyes wide with curiosity and a hint of apprehension. "Vikram, what exactly does this prophecy entail? What does it mean for us?"

Vikram looked at each team member, weighing his words carefully. "The prophecy speaks of a cosmic alignment that, if left unchecked, will tear open the fabric separating our world from the divine. Such an event could unleash chaos on an unprecedented scale. It's written in ancient texts, hinting that when the realms converge, chaos and disturbances will be unleashed upon the earth."

The room fell silent as each team member absorbed the gravity of Vikram's words. The air was thick with a sense of impending urgency.

Maya, perched on the edge of her seat, glanced at Vikram. "What's the prophecy about?" she asked, her voice tinged with both excitement and apprehension.

Vikram nodded and gestured to a set of ancient texts laid out before them. "The prophecy speaks of a cosmic disruption, a cataclysmic event that threatens to upset the balance between the mortal and mythological realms. It's written in ancient texts, hinting that when the realms converge, chaos will be unleashed upon the earth."

The room was filled with thoughtful silence as each team member absorbed the gravity of Vikram's words. The air was thick with a sense of impending urgency.

Anjali, breaking the silence, leaned forward, her brow furrowed in concentration. "This convergence—could it be what's causing the anomalies we've been noticing? The patterns and shifts in energy we've detected?"

Vikram nodded. "Exactly. The texts describe a point where cosmic energies align. These energies, if not properly managed, could lead to catastrophic outcomes."

The weight of his words settled over the group, each member feeling the gravity of their discovery.

A single beam of light danced across the artifact's surface, creating intricate shadows of the ancient symbols etched into its metal skin. It was sitting on a table in the middle of the dimly lit room. The symbols seemed to have a life of their own and were whispering secrets from a very long time ago. There was a strong smell of old paper and excitement in the room as Vikram's team gathered around, ready to figure out what these mysterious marks meant.

Maya leaned over the artifact and traced the serpent's curves with her finger. Her eyes were wide with interest. She pointed to the first symbol, "The Coiled Serpent." This symbol looked like a serpent winding around itself in a beautiful design that changed appearances when looked at from different angles. Its scales are very detailed, showing how graceful and flowing a serpent is.

In Hindu and Buddhist mythology, the serpent represents the Naga gods, who are thought to guard secret knowledge and treasures. The coiling serpent stands for birth, renewal, and the way that life and death happen in cycles. It is often linked to Kundalini energy, a spiritual force that rests at the base of the spine but can be woken up by meditation and awareness.

Rohan, leaning over the table, added with a scientific gleam in his eye, "And it's a testament to the universality of these patterns. Look at the spiral—it mirrors DNA, the building blocks of life. The ancients might have understood concepts we are only now beginning to grasp."

From a scientific point of view, the coiled serpent looks like the double helix structure of DNA, which stands for genetic potential and evolution. It can also stand for electromagnetic fields, which suggests that the artifact might be able to use or change these forces. The shape of the spiral suggests a link to natural events like galaxies, hurricanes, and even the mathematical Fibonacci sequence. This suggests that the spiral is connected to the basic patterns that rule the universe.

As the group looked at the artifact, Anjali pointed to the next sign, which was the Interlocking Triangles. The triangles on the artifact were carved with great skill, creating a complicated geometric pattern that looks like the Star of David or the old Hindu symbol Shatkona. The triangles meet in a way that looks good, making a star with six points that seem to be full of energy.

"These are more than just decorative elements," she said, her voice filled with awe. "They represent the ancient idea of balance—opposites in harmony, just like Shiva and Shakti."

Maya nodded, eyes fixed on the symbol. "It's a universal concept found in many traditions—the Yin and Yang, the balance of creation and destruction. It's about finding equilibrium in the chaos."

Vikram pondered this, connecting the symbol to scientific concepts. "Think about it in terms of chemistry," he suggested. "The triangles could represent stable molecular bonds—structures that withstand immense pressure because they balance opposing forces."

Rohan chimed in with enthusiasm, "And in physics, it's like the duality of particles and waves—two states that coexist, defining the behavior of matter and energy. These triangles could hold the key to understanding how these forces work together."

Raj, thoughtfully observing, added, "The symbol might be a guide—a way to align our scientific endeavors with the wisdom of the past, blending what we know with what we can only begin to imagine."

Together, they realized that the triangles that fit together were a strong symbol—a mix of mythological and scientific ideas that told them to look for balance and understanding as they tried to figure out what the artifact was all about.

The third sign caught Maya's eye as the team looked at the Celestial Bodies sign. The sign was carefully carved into the artifact and showed the sun, moon, and stars in a balanced way. The center is where the sun is, and its highly detailed rays reach outward. There are crescent moons and groups of stars all around it, carefully placed to give the impression of movement and order in the universe.

"This is fascinating," Maya said, tracing the sun's rays with her finger. "In mythology, the sun is often seen as a source of life and power, a force that connects all living things."

Anjali added, "And the moon signifies the passage of time, the ebb and flow of life. It's a reminder of the cycles we all go through, both in nature and in our personal journeys. The sun is seen as a symbol of life, energy, and creation, while the moon represents change, intuition, and the cyclical nature of time. Stars are frequently viewed as the souls of ancestors or guides through the dark night. Together, these symbols represent the eternal dance of light and darkness, the balance between the known and the mysterious, and the interconnectedness of the universe."

Vikram nodded, considering the scientific angle. "From an astronomical perspective, this symbol could represent the balance of forces that govern our universe—gravity, light, and the delicate interplay of celestial bodies."

"The sun is the center of our solar system, providing energy and sustaining life. The moon's phases influence tides and biological rhythms, while stars are distant suns, each with its own planetary systems and potential for life. This symbol could represent the artifact's connection to celestial mechanics, suggesting a profound understanding of astronomy, gravitational forces, and the potential for harnessing cosmic energy," said Raj, looking closely at the symbol.

Rohan, always eager to explore the scientific implications, suggested, "Perhaps this symbol holds clues to the artifact's potential. It could be a map of celestial alignments or a guide to harnessing energy from these cosmic bodies."

Raj, pondering the deeper meaning, concluded, "It's a testament to the ancients' understanding of the universe—a blend of myth and science that challenges us to explore the connections between our world and the cosmos beyond."

The team was amazed at how complicated the fourth symbol on the artifact was as they looked at it. It was the Kalpavriksha sign. The item showed the Tree of Life as the Kalpavriksha. It was a beautiful tree with a wide canopy that stood for wealth and plenty. Its roots went deep into the ground, and its branches, which were full of fruit and flowers, reached high into the sky. The leaves sparkled with complicated patterns, and at the base of the trunk, there were small carvings of mythical creatures and gods that made it look like it was holy.

Maya traced the lines of the roots with her finger, saying, "The Kalpavriksha is more than just a tree; it's a cosmic symbol of fulfillment and wisdom. It connects the earth to the divine, offering endless possibilities."

Anjali added, "In mythology, it serves as a bridge between the material and spiritual realms. This depiction reminds us that knowledge and resources are interconnected, just like the tree's roots and branches. Often associated with the gods and the heavenly realms, the Kalpavriksha is a symbol of prosperity and spiritual enlightenment. It emphasizes the interconnectedness of all life and the unity between the physical and spiritual worlds."

Vikram pondered the scientific aspects, suggesting, "This might symbolize the genetic tree of life, showing how everything in nature is interdependent. The idea of a wish-fulfilling tree aligns with the potential to unlock new scientific discoveries through understanding life's complexities."

Rohan, intrigued by the potential applications, said, "Perhaps this artifact contains clues to harness natural energies or biotechnologies that mimic nature's abundance. It could guide us toward sustainable solutions by understanding ancient knowledge."

Raj, reflecting on the dual symbolism, concluded, "The Kalpavriksha as the Tree of Life is a perfect blend of mythology and science. It challenges us to explore its secrets and find ways to use this knowledge to benefit humanity."

As the team moved on to the last symbol, the Ouroboros symbol on the artifact, a sense of profound significance washed over them. Maya studied the symbol closely, saying,

"The Ouroboros is one of the most ancient symbols, representing the endless cycle of life and death. It's fascinating how different cultures saw it as a marker of continuity and renewal."

Anjali nodded in agreement. "In Hinduism, it reflects the cycle of samsara, the eternal cycle of reincarnation. It's a reminder that life is an endless journey and everything is interconnected."

Vikram added, "From a scientific standpoint, the Ouroboros could represent closed-loop systems in nature—how life sustains itself through cycles. It could hint at an advanced understanding of the universe's inner workings. It might symbolize the closed-loop systems found in nature and the universe, such as the water cycle, the carbon cycle, or even the process of DNA replication. It could suggest an advanced understanding of physics and biology, portraying concepts of energy conservation, entropy, and the cyclic nature of matter and energy in the cosmos."

Rohan stood at the forefront, his eyes glued to the digital map displayed on his tablet. "I've been analyzing the artifact's chemical composition," he began, swiping through various screens. The excitement in his voice was palpable. "It's unlike anything found in our periodic table—a unique alloy that seems to react with electromagnetic frequencies. These properties could mean it acts as a conductor for cosmic energies."

His words hung in the air, making people curious. The strangely shiny artifact seemed to pulse slowly, as if it knew they were looking at it.

Anjali, always the inquisitive scholar, leaned in closer. Her eyes sparkled with curiosity. "And let's not forget the mathematical symmetries encoded in the inscriptions," she added, pointing to the geometric patterns etched onto the artifact's surface. "The geometric patterns aren't just decorative—they're equations. They describe cosmic events, aligning with significant historical catastrophes."

She paused, allowing her words to resonate. Her mind raced with possibilities, linking each pattern to events etched into the fabric of history.

Raj, who had been poring over a stack of ancient texts, nodded in agreement. His voice was steady and thoughtful. "We've identified connections between these inscriptions and various myths," he said, tracing a finger over one of the texts. "The mathematical sequences match those found in texts describing the Yugas—the cyclical epochs of time in Hindu cosmology."

The team exchanged glances, each of them absorbing the gravity of Raj's revelation. The room felt charged with the weight of understanding ancient truths that had long been hidden.

Maya, the historian with a penchant for mythological parallels, leaned forward, her face illuminated by the glow of the digital projection. Her insight was critical, bridging the gap between history and science. "So, the myths about Vasuki and the churning of the ocean—Samudra Manthan—aren't just stories. They're historical accounts of these cosmic disruptions. Vasuki, as the churning rope, symbolizes the delicate balance of forces that, if misaligned, could wreak havoc."

When she spoke, there was a quiet moment as the team thought about how huge what they had found was. It was like the item was whispering its secrets to them, and they were the ones who could understand them.

As they put all of these symbols and other pieces of information together, a story began to take shape. The artifact wasn't just a relic; it held old knowledge that connected science and myth. The team took a moment to feel how important the moment was.

Vikram stood at the head of the table, the artifact before him like a puzzle waiting to be solved. "We've been chasing fragments of history and science," he said, his voice resonating with the gravity of their task. "Now, we stand at the brink of a revelation—one that speaks of a prophecy with the power to alter the very fabric of our world." As each sign was figured out, the room went into a quiet state of reflection. The puzzle parts were coming together to make a more complete picture that included both spiritual and scientific ideas.

Vikram unfurled an ancient scroll, its surface covered in faded script and symbols matching those on the artifact. "The prophecy," Vikram read aloud, "foretells of a time when the cycles of the earth will falter, and the balance between the mortal and the mythological will be disrupted. A cataclysmic event shall arise, borne from the sins of hubris and the neglect of ancient wisdom."

The words echoed in the room, their meaning sinking in like a heavy stone dropped into a still pond.

Maya (speaking softly, her voice filled with a mix of awe and trepidation): "This is a warning and a call to action."

We've learned that the myths we've studied are more than just stories. They teach us how to keep the divine and our world in balance."

Anjali (her analytical mind racing, began connecting the dots): "If the artifact's inscriptions are correct, these ancient cosmic disruptions align with historical events. Each epoch, or Yuga, is marked by massive upheavals—natural disasters and shifts in human civilization. The signs are here again, and they point to another imminent cycle."

Rohan (pulling up data on the chemical composition of the artifact): "The alloy's reaction to electromagnetic frequencies suggests it might have been designed to communicate or control cosmic energies. Imagine a device that taps into the planet's energy cycles, stabilizing or even amplifying them."

Anjali (cross-referencing astronomical data, nodded in agreement): "The interlocking triangles and celestial symbols aren't random. They map out stellar alignments and gravitational influences. If we can interpret these correctly, we could predict—and possibly prevent—these cataclysmic events."

Anjali (deeply engrossed, highlighted the mathematical correlations): "The equations inscribed here correlate with natural cycles and cosmic events. They predict a series of alignments leading to a potential collapse, a breakdown of the Earth's natural harmony."

Rohan (typing furiously on his laptop, confirmed her findings): "These patterns match those of significant past events—major earthquakes, tsunamis, and even climate shifts. The artifact is a record, a predictor of these cosmic cycles."

Maya (her voice steady yet filled with urgency, concluded): "It's a warning. The myths we've studied aren't mere stories; they're guides to maintaining this delicate balance. The prophecy is a call to action—a reminder of our responsibility to heed the lessons of the past."

The room buzzed with a mix of excitement and concern as they processed the revelation.

Raj, bringing his historical knowledge to bear, elaborated, "In the Yugas, each epoch ends in upheaval, cleansing the world for renewal. The prophecy might not only be about doom but about transformation—a chance to correct our course."

Vikram, synthesizing the group's insights, spoke with conviction. "We stand at a precipice where myth and science converge. This artifact is more than a relic; it's a guide. Our mission is to bridge the gap, using this ancient wisdom alongside modern technology to avert disaster and preserve the balance."

As it dawned on them, the team realized how important their task was. They were not just students; they were guardians of a long-lost tradition who were responsible for keeping the future safe. There was a sense of new intensity in the air in the room. Shadows flickered in the dim light, making it look like ancient spirits were there to witness the discovery. The artifact was no longer just an antique; it had turned into a lighthouse that led them to their destination.

Vikram closed the scroll with a decisive snap, his expression resolute. "We must decode the remaining mysteries this artifact beholds."

His words hung in the air, and the group felt like they were wearing a heavy coat because of what they meant. Each of them felt the pull of history and the duty that came with it.

The team, which used to be made up of different people, had come together to work toward a common goal. They knew that their quest wasn't just about finding the truth; it was also about stopping a disaster that could change the course of history.

Rohan, always the pragmatist, tapped on his tablet, bringing up a complex web of data. "If this artifact truly interacts with cosmic energies, we need to explore its scientific implications. I'll work on modeling how its electromagnetic properties might influence Earth's magnetic fields. We need to understand its potential impact on a global scale."

Anjali, flipping through a hefty tome, added, "And I'll continue decoding the inscriptions. There may be hidden layers of meaning in the text—perhaps clues that could guide us on how to use or counteract the artifact's power."

Raj, ever the historian, leaned over to study the scroll. "I'll focus on finding historical parallels. There must be records of similar events in the past. Understanding how they were handled or mishandled might offer us insight into our next steps."

As Vikram stood in the middle of the room, he looked over at his team's faces, which were lit by the lights from their computers and the candles on the tables. The air was thick with anxiousness and the weight of duty. The artifact, which was lying on the table like a sleeping giant, seemed to have a life of its own and be telling them things that only they could hear.

He felt a flood of thanks and pride that rose up inside him like a tide. Not like any other team, this one was his. They were more than just coworkers; they were a symphony of intelligence and insight, a mix of different skills that made them a powerful force.

"This is where myth meets science," Vikram said, his voice carrying the weight of his conviction. "Our strength lies in our ability to bridge these worlds."

He looked from Rohan, who was deeply focused on studying electromagnetic waves on his tablet, to Anjali, who was carefully reading the old writings with a burning determination. Raj was deep in his historical books, looking for similarities that would help him understand and make decisions. Maya, on the other hand, was making connections between mythology and the patterns that they had found in their study.

They were all working toward the same goal, which went beyond the limits of their individual fields. Vikram knew that each of them was an expert in their own field but that together they were trailblazers and explorers about to find facts that could change the course of history.

"Let's harness that power," he urged, his words a rallying cry that resonated in the hearts of those gathered. "Let's do it."

When he spoke, the room seemed to come alive with a physical energy and a sense of purpose that gave everyone more energy. It seemed like the universe had worked together to bring them to this point, give them the treasure, and trust them to keep its secrets safe.

Rohan, usually the skeptic, looked up from his data with newfound belief in the possibilities that lay before them. "If we can understand how these electromagnetic properties interact with Earth's magnetic fields, we might predict—and prevent—the disturbances the prophecy warns about."

Anjali added, her eyes alight with academic fervor, "The geometric patterns are equations that align with historical catastrophes. We're not just deciphering language; we're interpreting thè mathematics of fate."

Raj nodded, his mind piecing together the intricate tapestry of past and present. "History has always shown us the cycles of rise and fall, creation and destruction. If we can decode how these epochs align with cosmic events, we might find a way to break the cycle."

Maya, ever the bridge between myth and reality, summed it up with quiet determination. "The stories of Vasuki and Samudra Manthan are warnings. They show us what happens when the cosmic balance is disturbed. We need to heed those lessons."

Even though they were arguing a lot, Vikram felt calm. Step by step, they were getting smarter and getting the power to do something about it. The artifact, which was once a mysterious relic, had turned into a sign of unity and purpose, leading them on a trip that connected the old and the new. There was a light, a task, and a way to get there all in one.

Vikram knew they were more than students when they were in that room with all the history and unknown things that could be found. They were in charge of protecting the future by carrying on an old tradition.

"Let's get to work," he said, his voice steady and full of promise. "We have a prophecy to unravel and a world to protect."

After that, the team got right to work on their study. Their minds were clear, and they were ready for whatever came next. They were guardians of knowledge and truth, and they worked together to find a new way forward, one where myth and science could weave together to make a tapestry of hope and rebirth.

The mood in the room became more charged with possibilities as the team worked. At the center of their work was the item, which stood watch over them as they tried to figure out what it meant. Vikram, Maya, Anjali, Raj, and Rohan were on a journey that was both a story of discovery and an attempt to figure out what existence was all about.

In the room, the sounds of old wisdom and new science seemed to dance together, creating a complicated web that linked the past and the present. It seemed like the universe had set them up to meet, bringing together their skills and interests to find a way forward. It would be a journey that would test their resolve, push their knowledge, and finally show the true power of the artifact they had grown to know so well.

There was the steady hum of computers, the rustling of paper, and the steady beat of people working hard in the room. The flow of ideas was like a river, with each branch adding to the overall flow of knowledge. The forecast, which had been so hard to understand at first, started to make sense as they thought about it and made connections.

Vikram stood at the helm, guiding the team with a steady hand and a mind that bridged the realms of myth and reality. His eyes scanned the papers and screens before him, filled with symbols and equations, ancient texts, and modern theories. "We're not just interpreting a relic," he said, his voice carrying the weight of both caution and inspiration. "We're deciphering a blueprint for the balance of our world."

He pointed to a sequence of symbols that spiraled around the artifact's surface. Each was unique, yet interconnected, forming a narrative that transcended time. "These symbols speak of cycles—destruction and renewal. It's a pattern that echoes through history and mythology."

Maya leaned forward, tracing her finger along the artifact's surface. Her eyes, alight with the fire of discovery, moved between the artifact and her notes. "The Kalpavriksha, or the Tree of Life symbol, embodies the interconnectedness of all things. Its roots stretch into the past, while its branches reach toward the future. It's not just a symbol—it's a map of existence itself."

Her voice softened, filled with a sense of wonder. "It suggests that our actions, however small, resonate through time. The choices we make now can affect the course of history."

Rohan, with his analytical mind and engineering prowess, examined the artifact's chemical composition. His screens displayed a multitude of graphs and spectral analyses. "The metal itself is an anomaly," he explained, his voice tinged with fascination. "It's a conductor for energies we're only beginning to understand. It reacts to electromagnetic frequencies, potentially acting as a key to unlocking cosmic events."

He leaned back, considering the implications. "This isn't just about preserving history. It's about understanding the mechanics of the universe, the forces that bind it together."

Raj sifted through historical texts, connecting the dots between ancient events and contemporary anomalies. His mind worked like a well-oiled machine, piecing together a puzzle that spanned millennia. "Every significant historical event, every mythological tale, aligns with these celestial cycles. The rise and fall of civilizations, the stories of gods and demons—they're all chapters in the same book."

He turned to the team, his voice filled with conviction. "We must read between the lines of history to prevent the mistakes of the past from repeating."

Every hour that went by, the symbols that had seemed mysterious at first started to make sense in a way that made their bones tingle. The team found the forecast by using careful scientific research, mythological interpretation, and combining mathematical patterns with data from the past and the present. It showed how important it is to keep the balance between the mortal and celestial worlds, and how quickly they needed to do their job to stop chaos and welcome a new age of enlightenment. They saw the prophesy, which was an intricate work of fate and choice:

In the era when the mortal and celestial realms align, A choice will determine the fate of all. Should the balance be disrupted, chaos will reign, And the world will be plunged into darkness. But if harmony is maintained, A new age of enlightenment will dawn, Bridging the ancient with the modern, The mythical with the scientific.

As they sat there in reverent silence, the team felt the weight of their task like a heavy burden. They weren't just scholars trying to figure out what a piece of history meant; they were guardians of an old tradition whose job it was to keep the future safe.

Vikram's voice broke the silence, filled with determination and hope. "We have a choice—to stand by as passive observers or to act as custodians of this fragile balance. We must decode the remaining mysteries and prevent this cycle from breaking."

Maya nodded, her eyes reflecting the determination in Vikram's words. "We have the tools, the knowledge, and the resolve. Together, we can ensure that the prophecy remains just that—a warning, not a reality."

The room was filled with the sounds of both old knowledge and new science, a symphony that led them forward. As they learned more about the secret, they realized that their quest wasn't just for school. It was a fight for the soul of their world, a quest to combine myth and science into a quilt of hope and renewal.

It used to be a mysterious item, but now it was a symbol of unity and purpose. It told them what to do, gave them a task, and made a promise: the future was in their hands. They forged a new road together that mixed the old and the new, the spiritual and the scientific. With the strings of their shared knowledge, it was of hope and renewal. A fight for the world's soul was going on outside, but no one knew about it because they were moving forward. The team worked hard because they had a clear goal.

Now that they knew their journey had just started, the team set to work with a new sense of purpose. They were guardians of knowledge and truth, and they worked together to find a new way forward, one where the ghosts of the past led the way to a bright and open future.

They would work together to find the right balance between history and fate, myth and reality, and make sure that the story of the prophecy stayed one of warning and hope instead of chaos and destruction. As the artifact watched over them and their combined knowledge led the way, they set out on a journey that would test their resolve, push their understanding, and, in the end, show them the true power of the artifact they had grown to know so well.

And as the night wore on and the dawn of a new day approached, they knew that they were not alone. They had each other, they had the knowledge of the ages, and they had the promise of a future forged in unity and purpose—a future that was theirs to shape.

Chapter 7: The Revelation

Vikram's office at the museum had floor-to-ceiling windows that let in the early morning sun. The room was filled with old books, artifacts, and the newest research papers, giving it a warm glow. Light from the sun danced over the worn edges of books and lit up the dust particles in the air, making the room feel almost holy. The room itself was a sanctuary of history and scholarship that showed how dedicated Vikram had been his whole life to solving the riddles of the past.

Vikram was sitting at his desk, which was filled with artifacts and sounds from long ago. His office was a mix of different cultures, and the past of people could be heard whispering from every corner. From the outside, the mess might have looked like too much, but Vikram saw each thing as important—a piece in the big problem of history that he was determined to solve.

The item, a strange artifact that stood out in this well-organized chaos, was in the middle of it all. It was a twisted shape that looked like a serpent, and the surface was covered with complicated symbols that seemed to have their own life. Two bright emeralds in the artifact's eyes caught the light and sparkled with old wisdom as if they knew the secrets they held.

Visions of fierce fights between gods and mythical creatures in the sky had been bothering Vikram for days. The visions were vivid and shocking. He saw worlds mixing and clashing, with no clear lines between them, like watercolors bleeding into each other on a wet painting. He had visions that were like puzzle pieces: they were all different but strangely familiar, and they gave him a strange feeling of déjà vu that made him feel both uneasy and calm at the same time. It was like his mind was trying to find a long-lost memory or secret that had been buried deep in his conscious mind.

The visions showed up out of the blue, like unwanted guests, and demanded his attention at the worst times, like during meetings while he was preparing for classes or in the middle of the night when he should have been sleeping. He kept seeing them over and over in his head, like silent movies. The intensity and vivid detail of them scared him.

Today was different, though. Something changed today while Vikram was sitting alone in his office, which was always a mess with old books and artifacts. The room was filled with a warm glow from the early morning light that came in through the windows. It was like nature herself was trying to show him the way. In this calm moment, clarity broke through his confusion like a flashlight in the dark, leading him to a truth he could no longer evade.

The visions that seemed so scattered at first started to come together into a logical story. It played out in the back of his mind with a clarity he had never felt before. He saw a picture that he had been unable to see for a long time as if the puzzle parts had finally come together.

He was sitting at his desk and looking at the item in front of him. It was a well-made artifact that seemed to have its own life. Its elegantly coiled shape looked like a serpent, and the complex symbols carved into its surface gave off a faint, otherworldly light. Two bright emeralds in the artifact's eyes caught the light and sparkled with old wisdom that called to him.

He felt the cool weight of the artifact in his hands as he thought about what it meant. He was starting to remember the past through it, and it was a link to his real self. A rush of memories hit him like the shore after the tide came back in. It was like a natural force that washed away the barriers of forgetfulness and showed the truth that was hidden beneath.

His mind was filled with images, each one stronger and more clear than the last. Suddenly, he remembered the divine world, the majesty of Lord Shiva, and the moment he agreed to walk among people. He thought back to the talk with the gods, the holy vow he had taken to keep the balance between worlds, and the love and sacrifice that his trip would require.

He felt like a veil had been lifted, showing a picture of truth that he had been missing for a long time. He was stuck in a place where time didn't matter and reality was just a faraway memory. The room around him seemed to fade away.

Vikram took a deep breath. The air around him felt charged with energy, like the whole world was holding its breath. He was shocked and amazed to discover that he wasn't just Dr. Vikram Nair, the famous and respected archaeologist and scholar who had spent his whole life trying to figure out the mysteries of the past. No, he was Vasuki, the heavenly serpent king who was meant to walk among humans and connect the worlds of myth and reality.

He realized it all at once, and it hit him like a lightning bolt. It sent a chill down his spine and made his skin tingle with understanding. The weight of this realization made his heart race. The two sides of his life crashed together in a powerful moment of truth that almost killed him.

At that moment, the lines between his mortal life and his divine mission came together, and he found himself at a fork in the road. With its complex symbols and hidden power, the artifact was definitely his work. It was a divine reminder of his goal to bring the world back into balance and harmony.

He now knew why he had been interested in the artifact in the first place; it had always seemed like more than just a historical find to him. In a world full of chaos and doubt, it was his anchor, his guide star. He was called back to his real purpose by the light, which also reminded him of the vow he had made in divinity.

Before Vikram closed his eyes, he let the memories sink in. Each one was a sign of the trip that was to come. The road was clear, but it was also full of problems and things he had to give up. But he felt ready—ready to accept who he really was, to use the power that had been given to him, and to live out his fate as Vasuki, the guardian of balance between realms.

Any longer, the weight of the artifact in his hands was just a feeling. It was a sign of the power and obligation he felt inside. Vikram felt a deep sense of peace and clarity of purpose as soon as he opened his eyes. The doubts that had been bothering him for a long time were gone.

Vasuki was his name, and he was the serpent king. His journey had just started. The artifact would help him find his way, and his strong beliefs would protect him. He was ready to face the difficulties that lay ahead and bring balance back to the world, which was desperately needed.

Vikram stood tall in the quiet sanctum of his office. He could feel the ancient power surge through him, a promise of the battles and wins that were yet to come. There was a rough path ahead, but he would cut through the chaos with love, sacrifice, and the knowledge of all time. He would lead both worlds to a future where harmony ruled.

He stood up quickly, and as he walked to the window, the chair scuffed against the wooden floor. The skyline of New York City stretched out in front of him, showing how creative and driven people can be. Even though he was surrounded by steel and concrete, Vikram felt a deep link to something much bigger—a complex web of life that went beyond time and space.

With his eyes closed, he let the memories come back to him. The image of his talk with Shiva played over and over in his mind. It was a turning point that now had new significance.

The respected serpent king Vasuki found himself in a place where humans could not go and where time was just a thread in the vast tapestry of existence. He was standing in front of Lord Shiva. This space in the sky was where the human and the divine met. It was a place where the very soul of creation hummed with life.

There was an ethereal light in the air that seemed to dance in time with Shiva's holy presence. His bright body was sitting on a beautiful lotus flower that floated peacefully above an endless space. The range of the universe could be seen in the petals of the lotus flower, which shone with an otherworldly color. As Vasuki got closer, his huge coils made a beautiful spiral on the floor of heaven, and he bowed his head in respect.

In this holy place, the sounds of creation played over and over again like a symphony. Each note was a reminder of the divine's limitless power and kindness. It looked like the stars were singing praises, their light mixing with the endless darkness of the universe to make a work of art that could only be seen in space.

"Lord Shiva," Vasuki began, his voice reverberating through the realm with a melodious resonance. It was a voice that carried the weight of eons, a voice that had witnessed the birth and death of worlds. Yet beneath the reverence lay a thread of uncertainty, a rare apprehension that tinged his words. "My time among mortals has been enlightening, but I fear losing my true self in the labyrinth of human existence. What if I forget who I am and my purpose?"

Shiva looked at Vasuki with eyes that could see into the infinite depths of the universe. These eyes had seen the beginning of creation and would see it end. His face was carved from the very essence of peace, and his look was one of deep compassion. His presence cast an ethereal light that made complicated patterns in the endless void. The shadows told stories of old myths and timeless truths.

"Vasuki, my loyal companion," Shiva replied, his voice a harmonious blend of thunder and whisper. It was a voice that could command the cosmos yet offered solace like the gentle caress of a breeze. "You possess the strength of the universe within you. Yet, should the time come when you find yourself adrift, this artifact shall guide you back to your essence."

Shiva stretched out his hand in a fluid motion, and an intricately designed artifact appeared from the very fabric of reality. Being around it was amazing; the thing seemed to be full of life and energy. The shape of the artifact was like Vasuki's own powerful body: it was coiled. It had old symbols carved into its surface, and each one lit up with a mysterious light that changed colors like the rainbow.

The patterns of the symbols dancing across the artifact's surface looked like the secrets of the universe were hidden in the stars. There were some that looked like holy geometry and others that looked like the natural cycles of life and death. It was a storehouse of cosmic information, proof that gods knew about the mysteries of the universe.

Two bright emeralds, each shining with a brightness that seemed to reach into the soul, were at the center of the artifact. These eyes on the artifact were alive with old knowledge. They watched and knew everything there was to know about the universe. They seemed to be in tune with a quiet song that talked about harmony and balance, as well as power and duty.

"What is its purpose, my Lord?" Vasuki inquired, awe-struck by the artifact's profound presence. His eyes reflected the artifact's light, capturing the depths of its mysteries and the promise of enlightenment.

Shiva's smile was soft, like the dance that always goes on between making things and destroying them, between love and war. Shiva spoke with the weight of divine truth when he said, "It holds the key to your memory and the restoration of balance in both the mortal and mythological realms." "When the lines between these worlds become fuzzy, and chaos threatens to tear everything apart, the artifact will bring back your memory and power." Its job is to bring back your memory and strength when the balance between the real world and the world of myths is in danger. The things Shiva said reminded Vasuki that it is her job to keep this careful balance.

Vasuki bowed his head in understanding, the enormity of his responsibility settling upon him like a mantle of destiny. His heart swelled with gratitude, and a renewed sense of purpose flowed through his veins. "I will cherish it, Lord Shiva. May I remain worthy of this responsibility!" His voice was a solemn vow, a pledge that resonated with the unwavering determination that defined his spirit.

Shiva's eyes stayed fixed, filled with a knowledge that knew no end and was not limited by time. He reached out and put a comforting hand on Vasuki's shoulder. The touch was as soft as a whisper, but it had the power of creation itself, reminding them of the bond that was stronger than all worlds and realities.

"Remember, the path of love and sacrifice is intertwined," Shiva intoned, his voice carrying the weight of divine truth.

"Let your heart guide you, for it is in love that true strength lies." Shiva's parting words highlighted the intertwined nature of love and sacrifice. This foreshadows the challenges Vasuki will face in his mortal life, where love will play a crucial role in guiding his actions. Shiva's touch, imbued with cosmic power, symbolized the strength Vasuki draws from this bond.

At that very moment, a deep bond was made between the god and the serpent. It was a bond that would last forever, going beyond the limits of death and myth. Vasuki felt a renewed sense of purpose as he rose, the item safely wrapped in his coils. This clarity drove away the shadows of doubt and fear.

He was ready to start a trip that would test his bravery and determination. It would cross myths and real events to create a tapestry of hope and renewal because the serpent king had a fire in his heart that was fed by love, sacrifice, and the hope of a future where the balance of the worlds would be kept.

Shiva and Vasuki stood at the edge of fate together, their souls dancing in a way that had cosmic meaning. There was a dance that would be remembered forever as a link between the divine and the human, between the god and the serpent, and between the past and the future.

In Vikram's office, the table was full of papers, sketches, and digital screens showing different sets of data. Maya, Anjali, Rohan, and Raj were sitting around the table with the rest of the team, talking about the latest results.

Vikram walked into the room, his mind still reeling from finding out who he really was. He could feel the heavy artifact in his hand. Its complicated shape and enigmatic energy constantly reminded him that he was both Dr. Vikram Nair and Vasuki, the divine serpent king. After taking a deep breath to calm down, he turned to face his team.

Maya was the first person to notice Vikram come in because she was sitting closest to the door. The team had always been inspired by her lively personality, and today was no different. She looked up from her notes, and her eyes were filled with worry and interest. "Vikram," she called out, her voice warm and inviting, "you look like you've seen a ghost. Is everything okay?"

Vikram managed a faint smile, the weight of his newfound knowledge evident in his eyes. "I'm more than okay," he replied, his voice tinged with awe. "I've remembered something—something important."

Anjali, who was always eager to uncover new information, leaned forward with keen interest. Her eyes, framed by stylish wire-rimmed glasses, shone with curiosity. "What is it?" she asked eagerly. "Is it about the artifact?"

Vikram nodded, his thoughts still racing. "Yes, it is. But it's also about me—who I really am." He paused, searching for the right words. He took a deep breath and revealed, "I am Vasuki, the divine serpent king. The artifact is not just a relic we study—it was created to awaken my memories and powers." His voice was calm but carried an underlying current of urgency.

Maya was the first to break the silence, her voice a blend of skepticism and concern. "Vikram, we've been through a lot, but this sounds … surreal. Are you sure you're okay? Maybe the stress is getting to you."

Anjali shook her head, adjusting her glasses as if trying to see Vikram more clearly. Her academic background made her naturally skeptical of anything that didn't come with evidence. "Vikram, we've all seen strange things, but claiming to be a mythical being? This isn't like you."

Rohan, the pragmatist of the group, leaned back in his chair, crossing his arms. "You've always had a wild imagination, Vikram, but this is a bit too far, don't you think? How can you expect us to believe this?"

Even Raj, who had just confessed his ties to the Order, looked bewildered. "I've seen extraordinary things, but how can you prove you're Vasuki?"

Vikram felt the weight of their disbelief like a physical barrier. He knew he needed to find a way to break through to them, to make them see the truth hidden beneath the veneer of the everyday world.

Vikram's heart pounded in his chest as he searched for the right words. The team's trust in him was crucial, and he couldn't afford to lose it now. "I understand how this sounds, but you have to trust me. I've had visions—memories—of my time as Vasuki. The artifact has awakened them, showing me who I truly am."

Maya frowned, her eyes searching his for any sign of deceit. "Vikram, we've known you for years. How could you be a deity and not know it until now?"

Vikram nodded, acknowledging her point. "I was sent here with my memories sealed to live as a mortal until the time was right. The artifact was a safeguard, a way to ensure I would remember when it was necessary."

Anjali sighed, clearly torn between her logical mind and the evidence that didn't fit into any logical framework. "You're asking us to take a huge leap of faith, Vikram. We need more than words."

Vikram felt a pang of desperation. He was losing them, and he couldn't let that happen. He needed something tangible, something undeniable. "I can show you," he said, his voice suddenly filled with resolve. "Give me a moment."

Vikram shut his eyes and focused on himself. Except for the soft hum of the city outside, the room was quiet. But in his mind, there was a lot of energy going around. He dug deep into himself to find the power that had been dormant for a long time. He saw his true form, the serpent coiling inside him, and the vastness of his being.

Thoughts made the room start to change. He was surrounded by a dim glow, and the room got cooler as a soft breeze blew through it. In answer, the artifact's light pulsed, and its emerald eyes lit up with a strange light. Papers were flapping around. The air was thick with the smell of old woods and the sound of thunder far away.

Vikram stood at the head of the table and took a big breath. His heart was beating fast with fear and purpose. He had never tried to use his divine skills while he was human, but now it was time to show who he really was.

"Watch closely," Vikram said, his voice steady but resonant with a newfound authority. "What I'm about to show you will be unlike anything you've ever seen."

His eyes were a deep brown color normally, but they seemed to get even darker and took on a shimmering color that sparkled like a serpent's scales. He briefly shut them, turned his attention inward, and called on the power that had been sleeping inside him.

The mood in the room changed a lot as Vikram focused. It got cooler, and the air felt like it had a force that was both old and new. A soft breeze moved through the room, moving papers around and messing up hair. It felt like reality itself was being stretched and remade.

When Vikram called out, the artifact on the table moved, and its emerald eyes lit up brighter, creating a greenish glow that lit up the room. Vikram's energy started to rise, and the symbols carved into its surface started to pulse in time with it.

Early on, Vikram's body changed so slowly that it was hard to notice. He got a faint glimmer on his skin, a soft glow that made the shapes of his body stand out. His back straightened, and he got bigger and more intimidating as if he were freeing himself from the limits of being human.

His neck and arms changed the most dramatically. There, faint patterns of scales started to show up, shimmering in the light like the skin of a magical serpent. His movements became smooth and graceful, and each one had a magical beauty to it.

It seemed like heat waves were wrapping around Vikram, making the air shimmer. From this distortion, the ghostly shape of a huge serpent started to take shape. It wrapped around him and was a clear but bright representation of Vasuki's true self.

The ghostly serpent's eyes were mesmerizing. They were two pools of green that looked just like the artifact's eyes. As if they were alive with ancient power and knowledge, they drew everyone in the room up to look at them. Vikram was a holy being, and these eyes showed more than just how he looked. They were like windows into his soul.

Maya gasped and took a step back as she stared in shock. Anjali grabbed the table and for a moment forgot about her doubts because of what she saw. Rohan sat up straight and looked at Vikram with wide eyes, as if he were seeing him for the first time; he being usually very calm.

Raj's expression shifted from disbelief to acceptance, the weight of his own revelations settling into a new reality. "This ... this isn't possible," he whispered, yet the evidence was undeniable.

Vikram opened his eyes, the glow around him subsiding, but the air still crackling with energy. "I am Vasuki," he repeated, this time with a certainty that resonated through the room. "And I need your help to fulfill my purpose."

Maya was the first to recover, her voice trembling slightly. "Vikram...or Vasuki...this is incredible. I can feel it—the energy, the power. It's undeniable. I don't know how to explain this, but I believe you. I've seen enough to know that not everything can be explained by science or logic." Her eyes were wide with admiration, reflecting the emerald glow of the serpent's gaze. She reached out instinctively as if trying to touch the ethereal form surrounding Vikram but pulled back, respecting the magnitude of the moment.

Anjali nodded slowly, still processing what she had witnessed. "I've always believed that history and mythology were intertwined in ways we couldn't understand. Maybe this is one of those ways. This defies everything we know about history and mythology," she said, her voice tinged with amazement. "Yet, it explains so much. The legends...

the stories…they were all pointing to this." She adjusted her glasses, her skepticism dissolving into curiosity and acceptance, her mind finally opening to the possibility of the myth made flesh.

Rohan uncrossed his arms, leaning forward with a newfound respect for Vikram. "Okay, I'll admit it. This is beyond anything I've seen. I always believed in what I could see and touch, but this…this is something beyond that. It's real, and it's here. If you're Vasuki, then we need to rethink everything we know." His pragmatic nature now accommodated a sense of wonder and respect for the unknown, acknowledging the presence of a force that transcended human understanding.

Raj, who had his own secrets to reveal, stood beside Vikram with a sense of solidarity. "I knew you were special, Vikram, but this…this is extraordinary. The Order doesn't stand a chance against what you are. We're with you, Vasuki. Whatever you need, we'll be there," said Raj in his thoughts as he could not still reveal the order.

His loyalty was clear, a bond built on trust and a shared goal, with his destiny now linked to the serpent king.

Vikram felt relieved as the tension in the room lifted, and his team accepted his truth. Though he knew the path ahead would be dangerous, their belief in him made him ready to face whatever challenges came.

The room was filled not with doubt but with unity and shared purpose. Vikram realized he couldn't do this alone, but now, with his team by his side, their loyalty strong, they would work together to restore balance to the world.

As the transformation faded, the serpent's image vanished, leaving Vikram in his human form. The room fell silent, but it was a silence of understanding and acceptance.

Vikram's heart filled with gratitude. He had feared rejection, but instead, he found unwavering support from his team, who now fully understood the importance of their mission.

"Thank you," Vikram said, his voice filled with sincerity and determination. "Together, we will face whatever challenges lie ahead. As Vasuki, I pledge to protect our world, and with your help, we can restore the balance that has been lost."

The team nodded together, their doubts gone. United, they were ready for the journey ahead, knowing it would test their courage and strength, but confident they were on the right path.

Now that they knew Vikram's true identity, the team felt a new sense of purpose. They were no longer just searching for artifacts and solving mysteries; they were part of a bigger story, one that connected the divine and the mortal. Together, they would fulfill their destiny, with Vasuki, the serpent king, leading them.

As they planned their next steps, Vikram let go of his past, focusing on the promise of the future and the strength of his true self. With his team by his side, Vasuki was ready to face the challenges of both the mortal and mythological worlds.

The journey had just begun, but Vikram—now Vasuki—knew that with love, courage, and conviction, they would succeed.

Chapter 8: The Confession

The conference room, usually filled with lively discussions, was now tense and quiet. Papers rustled softly on the table as Raj, the quiet support of the team, prepared to share a secret that had burdened him for a long time.

He stood up slowly, his heart racing as he faced his colleagues—friends who had become like family. His usual confidence was replaced by visible unease, and he took a deep breath, readying himself for the revelation.

"I need to tell you all something," Raj began, his voice steady but laced with underlying tension. "I've been involved with a secret society—the Order of the Ecliptic."

The words hung in the air, heavy with meaning, spreading shock and confusion like ripples in a still pond.

Rohan, sitting across from Raj, was the first to react. He leaned back in his chair, crossing his arms, his face a mix of disbelief and anger. Rohan had always been the skeptic, needing proof before he could believe.

“A secret society?” Rohan echoed, his voice dripping with skepticism. “What are you talking about, Raj? This sounds like something out of a conspiracy theory novel.”

Rohan’s eyes narrowed as he studied Raj, looking for any sign that this could be a joke or misunderstanding.

Maya, sitting next to Rohan, was clearly shocked. Her eyes widened, and she leaned forward, hands clasped in her lap as if trying to find some stability in the confusion.

“Raj, I can’t believe what I’m hearing,” Maya said, her voice a mix of disbelief and concern. “How long have you been involved with them? And why? This isn’t like you. How did you get mixed up in something like this?” Her tone was laced with disappointment, a reflection of the trust she had placed in Raj, now seemingly shattered by this unexpected confession.

Anjali, always the scholar, frowned in concentration. Her mind raced to understand the implications of Raj’s revelation, adjusting her glasses as she often did when deep in thought.

“You’re saying there’s a group out there with designs on the artifact, willing to exploit its power without understanding the full consequences?” Anjali’s voice was calm but tinged with urgency, each word carefully chosen as she sought clarity amidst the confusion.

Her analytical mind pushed her to fully understand the situation and how such a secret could remain hidden for so long.

Vasuki, standing at the head of the table, felt uneasy. His connection to Raj went beyond work; it was personal, built on shared experiences and respect.

"Raj, this is serious," Vasuki said, his voice carrying a tone of concern and leadership. "You're telling us that there's a group with intentions that could threaten not only our work but possibly much more?" His mind raced with the potential ramifications; each thought a stark reminder of the precarious path they were treading.

Raj took another deep breath, his gaze sweeping the room, meeting the eyes of each team member. He knew the gravity of his confession and the betrayal they must feel. Yet, he also knew it was time for the truth to come out, no matter the cost. "Yes," he replied, nodding. "The Order recruited me because of my skills in archaeology and linguistics. At first, they presented themselves as protectors of history, claiming they wanted to safeguard artifacts like the one we've been studying. It seemed noble, aligned with my own passion for preserving our past."

He paused, allowing his words to sink in before pressing on. "But over time, I began to see their true intentions. Their goal is not preservation but control—control of knowledge, of power. They believe that by harnessing the artifact's abilities, they can shape the future to their liking."

The room fell silent as everyone processed the revelation. It felt like a betrayal, but also a plea for understanding and redemption.

Rohan's skepticism started to fade, replaced by a reluctant recognition of the seriousness. His frown deepened, but a hint of empathy showed in his eyes. He uncrossed his arms, his posture softening as he tried to make sense of the new information.

"And now you want out?" Rohan asked, his voice softer though still tinged with disbelief. "You're saying you realized what they're about, and you're done with them? You've seen enough to know they're dangerous, and you've decided to walk away?" Rohan's mind raced with questions, yet beneath his skepticism lay a burgeoning respect for Raj's courage to break ties with such a formidable group.

Raj nodded, relief mingling with his lingering apprehension. "Yes. I've realized their intentions are dangerous, and I can't be part of it anymore. They're powerful, and they won't hesitate to remove anyone who stands in their way."

Maya's initial shock gave way to empathy as she considered Raj's predicament. She had always been able to see the heart behind people's actions, and now she saw Raj's vulnerability.

"Raj, it must have been hard to keep this a secret," Maya said softly, her voice filled with compassion. "You were stuck in a difficult position, but I'm glad you've chosen to come clean. We're here for you."

Her words were a lifeline, a reminder that despite the gravity of his confession, Raj was not alone.

Anjali remained focused, her intellectual curiosity driving her to probe deeper into the nature of the threat they faced.

"What exactly do they know about the artifact?" Anjali inquired, her voice laced with the urgency of a scholar desperate to connect the dots. "Do they understand its true power?"

Her questions were direct, aimed at uncovering any advantage they might hold over the Order, any knowledge that could tilt the scales in their favor.

Vikram watched as his team grappled with Raj's confession, their emotions a mix of betrayal, curiosity, and support. As the leader of this eclectic group, he felt a renewed sense of responsibility.

"This isn't just a matter of protecting the artifact anymore," Vikram said, his voice resonating with determination. "We're facing a group willing to go to any lengths for power. We must be ready to defend what's right and ensure the artifact doesn't fall into the wrong hands."

His words galvanized the team, a rallying cry that cut through the tension and united them in a common cause.

Raj felt a wave of relief wash over him, the burden of his secret finally lifted. The understanding and acceptance of his team provided a solace he hadn't anticipated.

"Thank you for hearing me out," Raj said, gratitude evident in his voice. "I know I've put you all in a difficult position, but together, we can face this threat and protect the world from the chaos they intend to unleash."

With Raj's confession out in the open, the team exchanged determined looks. They felt the weight of their responsibility but also the strength of standing together against a common enemy.

They were no longer just archaeologists and scholars; they had become warriors in a hidden battle.

In a secret chamber beneath the busy streets of Vienna, the leaders of the Order of the Ecliptic met urgently. The underground lair, dark and still, contrasted sharply with the lively city above, its shadows distorting reality.

The room was dim, with flickering candles casting an eerie light on the stone walls covered in arcane symbols and tapestries depicting the Order's past deeds. The air was thick with the scent of incense and a sense of unease. In the center stood a long, polished wooden table marked by the scars of many secret meetings.

Elder Matthias Richter, the Keeper of Secrets, sat at the head of the table, commanding attention and respect. His silver hair and piercing eyes gave him a timeless authority. Dressed in a robe embroidered with mysterious symbols, he embodied the Order's enigmatic and fearsome reputation.

He tapped his fingers rhythmically on the table, a subtle indication of his impatience and displeasure. The news of Raj's defection had hit him like a dagger, challenging the stability and secrecy of their plans. His eyes narrowed as he addressed the gathered members, his voice resonating with cold, calculated menace.

"In Shadows, We Illuminate."

"In Secrets, We Protect."

"This defection cannot be tolerated," the Keeper declared, each word meticulously enunciated to convey his disdain. "Rajan Mehta has chosen his side, and he will pay the price for his betrayal."

The room remained silent, the weight of the keeper's words sinking into the consciousness of each member present. They all knew the consequences of disloyalty, having witnessed the Order's ruthless handling of traitors in the past.

"We must act swiftly," Contessa Isabella Rossi said, her tone imbued with urgency and a hint of disdain for Raj's perceived foolishness. "The artifact must not fall into the hands of those who do not understand its true potential. It is not just a relic of power; it is a key to unlocking dimensions beyond mortal comprehension."

She paused, letting her words settle like a storm cloud about to burst. The others listened closely, knowing Rossi's reputation for sharp insight and strategic thinking. Her advice was seldom wrong and held great influence within the Order.

Lady Eleanor Blackwood sat near the Keeper, her eyes reflecting a cunning intelligence. "We have ways to ensure compliance and retrieve what's ours," she added, her voice calm but firm. "Raj's knowledge of the artifact's location and capabilities makes him a liability we cannot afford."

Her words were calm, spoken with the confidence of someone skilled in manipulation and control. Blackwood's mind was a maze of schemes, always ahead of any opponent.

The leaders of the Order continued debating, a mix of frustration and determination in their voices. The room felt smaller, the shadows seeming to listen closely to the secrets unfolding.

The Keeper leaned forward, his gaze fixed on Rossi and Blackwood. "We need to recover the artifact before Raj and his allies can fully comprehend its significance. Our operatives must be deployed to monitor their movements, and contingency plans should be set in motion."

His voice was powerful, emphasizing the urgency of their mission. The artifact symbolized not only power but the core of their influence in the hidden world they aimed to dominate.

Sir Alistair Donovan nodded in agreement, his mind already working through the logistics of the task ahead. "I'll consult the Oracles. Their guidance can illuminate paths we might otherwise overlook. As for Raj, his betrayal will be his downfall. We must remind him that there is no escaping the reach of the Order." His words dripped with an ominous promise, a reminder of the Order's relentless pursuit of those who dared to defy them. He turned to Eleanor, her expression one of determination. "Julian, your expertise will be crucial in deciphering any moves Vikram's team might make. We need to anticipate their actions and counter them before they gain any advantage."

Eleanor Blackwood gave a slight nod, her mind already calculating possibilities and probabilities. "Rest assured, our network of informants and our mastery of ancient texts will give us the edge we need. Raj may have turned against us, but he is just one piece in a much larger game."

The room grew darker as Eleanor spoke, the candlelight casting long shadows that seemed to move on their own. Each leader of the Order knew the gravity of the situation and the need for quick action.

The meeting ended with a silent understanding: subtlety was no longer an option. As they stood, their faces showed a grim resolve.

The Order of the Ecliptic, a secretive and powerful society, had been challenged. They would stop at nothing to reclaim what they believed was theirs.

As the Keeper left the chamber, he paused, his gaze lingering on the symbols carved into the stone walls—representing power, control, and the destiny he believed awaited the Order. The silence in the room underscored the seriousness of their mission, reminding him that their strength and salvation lay in the shadows.

With a final, determined glance, the Keeper exited, his footsteps fading into the hidden sanctuary. The Order was moving, and soon the world would feel the effects of their pursuit. The meeting ended with a silent agreement: being cautious was no longer an option. As they got up, their faces showed serious determination. The Order of the Ecliptic, a secretive and powerful group, had been challenged. They would do whatever it took to take back what they believed was rightfully theirs.

The office slowly emptied, leaving only the hum of the air conditioning and the rustle of papers as the last team members left. The setting sun's golden light poured through the large windows, casting long shadows across the floor. Vikram and Maya stayed behind, lingering in the quiet after their intense meeting.

Maya stood by the window, the amber light creating a soft glow around her. She turned to Vikram, her eyes showing both wonder and concern. For a moment, they were silent, letting the day's revelations sink in.

Vikram turned to Maya, his face gentle but determined. His eyes reflected a mix of ancient knowledge and the vulnerability of new discoveries. He felt torn between two worlds, balancing his mortal life with his divine nature.

Maya met his gaze with a steady look, her eyes bright with both understanding and a touch of mischief that always seemed to reassure him. "So, you're a mythical serpent king. That's a twist I didn't see coming," she teased gently, a smile playing on her face.

Vikram chuckled, a sound that broke the tension and brought a lightness to the moment. "I've lived two lives, but until now, they've never converged like this. It's like awakening from a dream and realizing the dream was real." He paused his expression, a complex weave of sadness and joy. "It's strange, Maya. I've always thought of myself as a man dedicated to history, to unraveling the mysteries of the past. But now I realize I'm also a part of that history. And in this storm of revelations, you've been my anchor, the constant I needed. Believe me, it was a surprise for me too. But knowing that you're with me makes all the difference."

Maya moved closer, her eyes never leaving his. She reached up, her hand tenderly cupping his cheek, the warmth of her touch grounding him in the present moment. "You're not alone, Vikram. We're all here for you, but especially me. Whatever comes, whatever challenges we face, I'm with you."

Maya stepped closer, her hand reaching up to trace the line of his jaw, her touch as gentle as a whisper. "Whatever comes, Vikram—or Vasuki," she added with a playful lilt, "I'm with you. We've faced mysteries before, but this one is special because it's ours."

Vikram took her hand in his, drawing strength from the simple contact. He marveled at her ability to face the unknown with such unwavering courage. "Maya, you've been my anchor, my compass. In all of this chaos, you keep me grounded. I don't think I could do this without you. You've always seen the truth of things, even when I couldn't."

Maya shook her head softly, her eyes serious now. "It's not just me, Vikram. Look around you. Anjali, Rohan, Raj—we're all doing this together. You don't have to carry this burden alone."

The mention of their friends brought Vikram back to the reality of their situation. He glanced toward the door, where Anjali had paused, sensing their conversation was nearing its end but reluctant to intrude.

Anjali, who had been gathering her notes, looked up with a curious smile. "Well, if you're planning on fighting secret societies and preventing apocalyptic disasters, you're going to need all the help you can get," she quipped. Her tone was light, but her eyes were full of sincerity. "We've got your back, Vikram."

"Indeed," Rohan chimed in, still seated at the table, tapping his pen thoughtfully against his chin. "Though I have to admit, I didn't foresee my archaeology career involving mystical artifacts and world-saving missions. But hey, it beats grading papers."

Raj stood by the wall, the weight of his earlier confession still settling in his mind. He looked at Vikram, his face a mix of guilt and gratitude. "I'm sorry I kept my involvement with the Order from you. I thought I was doing the right thing, but I see now how wrong I was. Thank you for still trusting me."

Vikram nodded, his expression understanding and forgiving. “We all have our paths to walk, Raj. What matters is that you’re here now, with us. We need every ally we can get.”

Maya nodded in agreement. “The Order underestimates what a group of determined friends can achieve. They’re not just up against a divine serpent—they’re up against all of us.”

The room filled with a renewed sense of camaraderie, each team member feeling the threads of fate weaving them closer together. They were no longer just colleagues or friends; they were a family united by a shared purpose.

As the sun set, filling the room with soft twilight, Vikram felt a deep sense of peace. The day’s revelations had been life-changing, challenging everything he thought he knew, but he was ready for whatever came next.

With Maya by his side and his team supporting him, he was confident they could overcome any obstacle. They would protect the artifact, fight the Order, and fulfill their destiny.

In that moment, as the world outside moved on, Vikram and Maya stood together, hand in hand, a symbol of light and hope in the growing darkness. No matter what came their way, they would face it together, united by love and strength.

As the last of the sunlight faded, Vikram and Maya shared a quiet moment, eyes locked in a silent promise. “Let’s do this,” Vikram said softly, determination etched in his voice.

Maya squeezed his hand, her expression fierce and loving. “Together.”

The room felt still as they stood together, surrounded by a quiet understanding and unspoken promises. The chaos of the outside world faded, leaving only the two of them in their own world.

Their eyes met, silently sharing their fears and hopes. Time seemed to slow, and the air felt heavy with unspoken vows.

As if drawn by an invisible force, they leaned in, their lips meeting in a soft, meaningful kiss. It was a promise, a union of worlds—mortal and divine, love and duty. The kiss spoke of loyalty and trust, a vow to protect each other and the world they loved, no matter the cost.

In that moment, they found balance, a harmony between the roles they were meant to play. For Vikram, it was a moment of clarity—a reminder that, despite his divine duties and the threats ahead, love was the strongest force. For Maya, it reaffirmed her belief in him, in both his human and divine sides.

The setting sun faded, casting a gentle twilight across the room. The day was ending, but for Vikram and Maya, a new chapter was beginning—one where they would face the unknown together, hand in hand, united in purpose and heart.

As they parted, still wrapped in the warmth of their moment, they knew they would face whatever came next with courage and love. In that certainty, they found peace, ready to take on the world and its challenges, knowing they had each other.

Chapter 9: Echoes of the Cosmic Realm

In the vastness of the cosmos, where stars were born and galaxies danced, existed the cosmic arena—a realm of endless possibilities and eternal conflict. It was beyond human understanding, where time and space merged, setting the stage for battles among divine beings. The laws of the physical world did not apply here. The sky was alive with vibrant colors and lights, while the ground was made of mist and celestial stone. The air hummed with the energy of creation and destruction, reflecting the immense power of those who inhabited this realm.

Mount Mandara stood as a towering pillar, its peak reaching the heavens and its roots buried deep in the unknown. It was here, amidst chaos and beauty, that Vasuki, the great serpent, readied himself to face his ancient foes in battles that would be remembered forever.

A storm of wind and thunder signaled the arrival of Indra, king of the gods. His chariot, pulled by horses whose manes crackled with electricity, descended in a display of power and grandeur. As he stepped forward, the very air seemed to tremble at his presence.

Indra was magnificent in his divine armor, decorated with jewels that reflected the power of storms—sapphires like rain-filled clouds and diamonds that sparkled like lightning. His presence radiated both majesty and authority, symbolizing his control over the skies.

Standing tall, with his crown glinting under the celestial lights, Indra addressed Vasuki, his voice echoing like the drumbeats of war. "Vasuki, you who coil around the world tree, constraining its growth with your chains of balance, do you not see? Progress demands the surrender of harmony to power. True rule lies in the hands of those who dare seize it."

Vasuki, coiled around the base of Mount Mandara, radiated ancient wisdom and calm, anchoring him in place. His shimmering scales reflected the light of distant stars and the colors of the cosmos. When he lifted his massive head, his eyes, as deep as the void yet glowing with inner fire, met Indra's—steady and composed.

"Indra," Vasuki spoke, his voice a deep rumble that resonated through the cosmic ether, "your vision is clouded by the lust for dominion. You mistake power for strength and tyranny for leadership. The cosmos thrives on balance, not the reckless pursuit of control. What you call chains, I call the threads that weave the fabric of reality."

His words were deliberate, each one reflecting the countless ages he had spent watching the universe's flow. Vasuki embodied patience, knowing that balance is essential for all things to endure.

Indra scoffed, his impatience flickering like the storms he commanded. "Balance is the refuge of the weak, Vasuki. It is the excuse of those too timid to wield the power at their fingertips. The universe does not reward restraint—it rewards the bold, the ambitious."

His eyes burned with the power of an approaching storm. Indra strongly believed in the righteousness of his cause, seeing himself as a force for progress, even if it meant causing upheaval.

Vasuki, unperturbed, replied, "And what of the consequences, Indra? Have you not learned from the devastation that follows when the scales are tipped too far? Ambition unchecked leads to ruin, not renewal. It is the balance that nurtures that allows the cosmos to endure and evolve."

The serpent's words held ancient wisdom, reminding of the cycles of creation and destruction that rule all things. Vasuki had seen countless worlds rise and fall, and his perspective was driven by the need to protect what was essential and true.

Indra's gaze narrowed, and his voice was fiercely determined. "The world must change to grow. The fires of ambition forge strength, and through strength, we attain greatness. The weak fall away, making room for the strong to rise. It is nature's way, Vasuki."

He gestured to the chaotic cosmic arena, a symbol of the power struggles that shaped reality. Indra saw himself as a necessary force, a bringer of change in a universe that resisted it.

"Nature's way is not chaos," Vasuki countered softly, his voice carrying the serenity of a still pond. "It is the dance of order and entropy, each step measured and purposeful. In your quest for greatness, you forget the foundation upon which it is built."

Indra laughed, the sound echoing like a thunderclap. "The foundation is meant to be shattered, serpent. From the rubble, new worlds will rise, greater than those that came before."

The tension between the two divine beings was intense, like the air before a storm. Their words, filled with conviction and old grudges, echoed through the cosmic arena, preparing for a confrontation that was both certain and significant.

Indra's ambition clashed with Vasuki's dedication to balance, reflecting their opposing natures. The air buzzed with energy, and the cosmos seemed to hold its breath, waiting for the battle ahead.

Vasuki, feeling the weight of his responsibility, spoke once more, his voice a solemn vow. "Then let us see, Indra, whether the cosmos favors the hand that reaches for power or the one that steadies it. Let us dance the dance of the elements and discover where true strength lies."

As his words echoed, the cosmic arena stirred. The ground trembled with the power of divine energies building for the clash. The skies darkened, and the winds howled—a celestial symphony preparing for the great battle.

Indra, with a fierce grin, raised his vajra, the mighty thunderbolt, and prepared to unleash the storm within him. "Very well, Vasuki. Let us see if your balance can withstand the fury of the storm."

Vasuki coiled tighter around Mount Mandara, his resolve as strong as the mountain. The cosmic energies surrounded him, showing his deep connection to the forces of creation. He was ready to protect the harmony he cherished from the storm of ambition that threatened to disrupt it.

With a powerful clash, the two divine beings began their battle, their powers colliding and shaking the very foundations of the cosmic arena. The air crackled with lightning, thunder roared, and the earth trembled beneath their strength. The arena became a stage for a battle that would be remembered forever.

Indra's lightning bolts struck like a fierce storm, each one showing his control over the skies. The air buzzed with electricity, casting flickering shadows as he unleashed his power with fury and precision.

Vasuki, despite his size, moved with surprising agility, dodging the bolts of energy. His scales gleamed with iridescent light, reflecting the cosmic forces as he skillfully deflected Indra's attacks.

The ground shook with each blow, and reality itself seemed to warp under the weight of their power. The cosmic arena echoed with their clash, a symphony of elemental forces that matched the heartbeat of the universe.

In the midst of their battle, both combatants had a moment of clarity—they realized their conflict was not just about power, but a reflection of the eternal struggle between order and chaos, creation and destruction.

Vasuki, tapping into the cosmic energies within him, found the balance where harmony and ambition could coexist. It was a delicate fusion of opposing forces, creating something greater than either alone.

With focused determination, Vasuki released a surge of energy that rippled through the cosmic arena. The force struck Indra with the weight of the universe, breaking his defenses and sending him stumbling.

The skies cleared, and the storm calmed, leaving Vasuki standing strong and unwavering. The cosmic arena witnessed his victory, a testament to the power of balance and the wisdom of harmony.

As the dust cleared and the battle's echoes faded, Indra stood up, his eyes filled with awe and respect. He had been defeated, not by sheer strength, but by a mastery of balance he had underestimated.

"You have shown me the strength of balance, Vasuki," Indra admitted, his voice devoid of the arrogance that had marked their earlier exchange. "Perhaps I was wrong to dismiss its power. There is wisdom in your ways that I had not seen."

Vasuki, ever gracious in victory, inclined his head. "And you, Indra, have reminded me of the importance of ambition and the potential for growth that lies within it. Balance is not the absence of change but the guiding hand that shapes it."

Their conflict, once filled with tension and hostility, had transformed into mutual understanding—a recognition that both balance and ambition had a role in the cosmos.

As Indra faded into the ether, Vasuki stayed in the cosmic arena, reflecting on the lessons of their battle. It had tested his resolve, his understanding, and his mastery over the elements. Through it all, he learned that the dance of balance is not fixed but dynamic—constantly changing and evolving.

The cosmic arena floated in the vast universe, where time and space intertwined in a swirl of energies. Stars shone brightly above, casting their glow on the arena's ground, which glimmered like a magical dance floor. This was a place of limitless potential, where the very fabric of existence was tested by the epic battles of divine beings.

At the center stood Mount Mandara, a majestic celestial pillar. Its peak disappeared into the heavens, while its roots reached deep into the infinite below. Here, the elements met, each seeking dominance but maintaining a fragile balance that reflected the delicate harmony of the universe.

In the midst of this cosmic theater stood Vasuki, the great serpent, protector of balance and harmony. His massive form, covered in shimmering scales, reflected the many colors of the cosmos. His presence radiated calm, masking the powerful storm within, a symbol of his role as the eternal keeper of balance.

Suddenly, the cosmic fabric rippled as a new force entered. Agni, the fire deity, charged into the arena like a supernova, his arrival marked by flames that reached the sky. His chariot, a blazing comet pulled by horses made of living flame, streaked across the horizon, leaving fiery trails behind.

Agni emerged from the flames, his form a blaze of divine energy. His skin glowed like molten metal, and his hair crackled with embers, moving to an unseen rhythm. He wore scarlet and gold robes, each fold alive with flickering flames—a symbol of his control over transformation. His eyes, glowing with the light of a thousand suns, locked onto

Vasuki with a mix of challenge and curiosity. They burned with Agni's intense nature and his constant desire for change. He was the embodiment of fire's dual power—both a creator and a destroyer, a force of renewal and destruction.

"Vasuki," Agni called out, his voice a crackling flame that echoed across the cosmic expanse, "keeper of the balance, you stand as a bulwark against the tide of transformation. Your restraint is a chain that binds you, preventing the universe from realizing its true potential. Can you withstand the inferno of change that seeks to reshape all that exists?"

Vasuki's eyes, deep as the cosmic ocean and filled with ancient wisdom, met Agni's fiery gaze. He spoke with a calmness that belied the turmoil within, his voice a soothing balm that spread through the arena. "Agni, you who embody the transformative power of fire, your zeal for change blinds you to the chaos it can unleash. Fire is indeed a force of transformation, but without balance, it becomes a force of destruction. It is the harmony of elements that allows creation to flourish."

The serpent's words reflected the wisdom of countless ages spent observing the cycles of creation and destruction in the cosmos. Vasuki understood the need for change but also saw the importance of preserving the balance that sustains life.

Agni laughed, a sound like the crackling of burning wood—filled with both amusement and defiance. "Balance is but a temporary state, Vasuki, an illusion maintained by those too fearful to embrace the fire's full potential. Transformation is the only constant, and it is through the crucible of change that the universe evolves."

His eyes sparkled with restless energy, like the flames that surrounded him. Agni saw himself as a vital catalyst—a force of evolution in a universe that resisted change.

Vasuki, unperturbed by Agni's fervor, replied, "Change without consideration leads to ruin, Agni. It is the unchecked flames that scorch the earth and leave only ashes in their wake. True transformation is guided by wisdom, tempered by restraint, and balanced by harmony."

The serpent's words reflected his role as a guardian of balance, a reminder of the many worlds he had witnessed rise and fall over time. Vasuki embodied patience and the understanding that balance is essential for survival.

The tension between the two deities grew, filling the air with a sense of impending conflict. The cosmic arena seemed to hold its breath, anticipating the clash of powerful forces that would challenge the very fabric of existence.

Agni's flames surged, enveloping him in a corona of incandescent fire. "Very well, Vasuki. Let us see if your balance can withstand the fury of the flame!"

With a powerful motion, Agni unleashed a torrent of fire—a force of destruction that charged toward Vasuki. The flames twisted and surged, hungry to consume everything in their path, driven by Agni's unstoppable will.

The air shimmered with heat as the firestorm rushed toward Vasuki, a wave of intense energy threatening to engulf him. The flames moved with a life of their own, each flicker showcasing Agni's power and the unstoppable force of transformation.

Vasuki faced the firestorm with the calm of endless experience. He moved through the flames with a grace that defied their chaotic nature, each movement a careful dance of precision and intent.

Tapping into the element of water, Vasuki summoned a torrent that surged across the arena, dousing the flames and calming their fury. The steam rose in thick clouds, symbolizing the clash of opposing forces, as water met fire in a hissing battle of defiance.

Agni's laughter echoed through the arena—a sound that mingled challenge with respect. "Impressive, serpent, but can you withstand the true fury of the flame?"

With a forceful wave, Agni summoned a towering column of fire that twisted and surged toward Vasuki, an unstoppable wave of destruction. The flames crackled and roared, an embodiment of Agni's fierce determination to strike.

Vasuki stood undeterred, his eyes shimmering with a mysterious inner light. Harnessing the full extent of his power, he summoned cosmic forces, his very essence drawing upon the primordial elements. Water and fire fused under his control, forming a glowing, radiant shield. As the blazing flames crashed into the barrier, a dazzling explosion of light erupted, filling the cosmic arena with a blinding brilliance, the clash of elemental forces echoing through the vast expanse.

The clash of elements unfolded like a symphony, a powerful and resilient dance that echoed the very heartbeat of the cosmos. The arena became a boiling cauldron of creation and destruction, each burst of energy a testament to the balance Vasuki had sworn to protect.

In a rare moment of clarity, Vasuki felt the pulse of harmony, a fleeting but profound understanding of the perfect equilibrium between fire and water. It was a delicate, fragile balance, but one that he could feel deep within. With a singular focus, he harnessed his will and guided Agni's flames, not as an adversary but as an ally. The wild vortex of fire shifted and transformed, unfolding into a breathtaking spectacle—a radiant fusion of elemental forces where fire and water embraced in a stunning dance of beauty and unity.

As the firestorm finally waned, Vasuki stood amidst the calm, untouched and unwavering. The air around him shimmered with the lingering echoes of the clash, but his presence remained steady, a quiet testament to his mastery. Agni, watching this display of strength and poise, felt a deep sense of respect for his rival. With a slow, acknowledging nod, he recognized the power of balance—a force even greater than the fiercest flames.

"You have tempered the flame, Vasuki," Agni conceded, his voice a blend of admiration and acceptance. "The harmony of elements is a force to be reckoned with. But remember, transformation is an eternal cycle, and the fires of change are ever-burning."

Agni's words resonated with a deep understanding, carrying the weight of a truth he had come to grasp: transformation, though necessary, must be tempered by wisdom and guided by balance. In Vasuki, he saw a kindred spirit—one who understood that harmony could thrive even amidst the turmoil of the cosmos.

As Agni's form slowly dissipated, dissolving back into the ether, Vasuki remained in the quiet aftermath of their encounter. The cosmic arena, once filled with the fierce energy of battle, now lay still. Vasuki stood in reflection, the lessons of their clash unfolding in his mind. The battle had tested his resolve, his understanding, and his mastery over the elements. He realized that balance wasn't a fixed state; it was a dance—constantly shifting, ever-changing, and evolving with the rhythm of the universe.

The cosmic arena shifted again, reshaping itself beneath the weight of an immense, unseen force. The stars above seemed to waver and dim, as if the very heavens were bowing in deference. A vast shadow unfurled, stretching across the celestial expanse, signaling the arrival of Varuna, the lord of the oceans. His presence swept through the cosmos like a deep, resonant hum, vibrating through the very fabric of existence. It was a sound that echoed in the core of the universe itself, a reminder of the vast, mysterious depths he ruled with quiet, unyielding power.

From the depths of the cosmos, Varuna emerged—an embodiment of immense power and quiet majesty. His skin shimmered like the surface of the sea beneath a moonlit sky, an ever-shifting canvas of blues and greens that seemed alive with movement. His robes, flowing like liquid water, cascaded around him in graceful waves, their gentle curves defying gravity itself. Varuna's eyes were as deep and unfathomable as the ocean's darkest reaches, reflecting ancient mysteries and the countless secrets hidden beneath its surface. He stood tall and regal, his presence radiating a profound wisdom that had been forged over eons. The waters churned and swirled around him, sending ripples across the arena that mirrored the timeless ebb and flow of the tides. The very air seemed to pulse with the essence of the sea—a refreshing, invigorating blend of salt and fresh currents, filling the space with life and energy.

Varuna's voice echoed through the arena like a rolling wave—filled with both challenge and curiosity. "Vasuki, guardian of the balance, the depths of the ocean hold secrets that even the cosmos cannot fathom. Do you think your balance can withstand the relentless currents of the unknown?"

The question lingered in the air, thick with the weight of Varuna's challenge. He was the very embodiment of the ocean's dual nature—both calm and violent, serene and tumultuous. His presence spoke of the hidden depths, the mysteries, and uncertainties that swirled beneath the surface, unseen and unknowable to most.

Vasuki faced Varuna with a calmness that masked the storm within. The great serpent coiled, his scales glinting with a soft, inner light that caught the colors of the cosmos as though reflecting the universe itself. He was a being of balance, a protector of harmony in a world where chaos often threatened to overwhelm. His unwavering presence stood as a testament to the delicate equilibrium he maintained, a constant in a universe that teetered on the brink of disorder.

"The ocean is indeed a force of mystery, Varuna," Vasuki replied, his voice steady and serene, "but without balance, it becomes a force of chaos. It is the harmony of elements that allows creation to flourish, ensuring that the unknown does not become destructive."

Vasuki's words resonated with the weight of ancient wisdom, each syllable carrying the depth of his role as a guardian of the cosmic order. He understood the profound power of the unknown, a force that could shape the world in ways both beautiful and destructive. It was a force that demanded respect, for in its depths lay the potential for both creation and ruin. But Vasuki knew that balance was the key to navigating this vast, untamed power—an unspoken truth that had guided him through the ages.

Varuna's laughter rumbled like the crashing waves of a tempest—a sound filled with both mirth and challenge. "Balance, Vasuki, is but a fleeting state. The ocean is ever-changing, its currents unpredictable, and its depths unfathomable. It is through embracing the unknown that we discover the true nature of existence."

His eyes, dark and enigmatic, mirrored the endless depths of the ocean, reflecting a belief that change and unpredictability were at the very core of the cosmos. Varuna saw himself as the keeper of ancient secrets, a quiet guardian of the unknown. He understood that within the vast, uncharted waters of existence, there was both danger and wonder—an ever-present potential for discovery and transformation. In his presence, the mysteries of the universe seemed both more distant and yet closer than ever, waiting to unfold in their own time.

Vasuki, unyielding in his resolve, replied, "The unknown is indeed a powerful force, Varuna, but without balance, it becomes a maelstrom that consumes all in its path. True wisdom lies in harmonizing the known with the unknown, creating a path of stability amidst chaos."

The serpent's words echoed with a profound understanding of the cosmic dance—a delicate balance between order and chaos, where harmony was the invisible thread that held the fabric of existence together.

Varuna extended his hand, and the ocean answered with a deafening roar. Waves surged forward like a living force, intent on consuming everything in their path. The currents twisted and writhed, wild and untamed, their power a direct reflection of the unknown, propelled by Varuna's unwavering will.

The arena transformed into a maelstrom of water and light as Varuna unleashed the full force of the ocean. The waves crashed around Vasuki, encircling him in a vortex of seething currents. The serpent's scales shimmered with a radiant light, reflecting the violent intensity of the water as he prepared for the trial ahead.

The currents were relentless, a reminder of the ocean's unyielding nature, a force driven by the vast and unfathomable mysteries beneath the surface. They sought to drag Vasuki under, testing his strength and resolve against the unknown.

But Vasuki was unshaken. He met the challenge with poise and grace, his form flowing through the water with a fluidity that seemed to defy the chaos of the storm. Each twist and turn was deliberate, a dance of precision and control. His movements spoke of mastery—an embodiment of the balance he had sworn to protect.

Tapping into the element of air, Vasuki summoned a powerful gale that swept across the arena, scattering the surging waters and calming the ocean's fury. The wind whipped through the space, rising in swirling clouds that seemed to pulse with energy. It was a force of defiance, a clash of opposing elements—air meeting water in a breathtaking display of balance and power, each one asserting its presence in a perfect, dynamic harmony. The very air hummed with the tension of the encounter, as though the wind itself was challenging the ocean to yield.

Varuna's laughter echoed through the arena—a sound like crashing waves filled with admiration for the serpent's resilience. "Impressive, Vasuki, but can you withstand the true fury of the ocean?"

With a powerful, sweeping gesture, Varuna called forth a massive tidal wave that spiraled toward Vasuki, a relentless vortex of water and fury threatening to engulf him. The waves crashed with a life of their own, wild and untamed, driven by Varuna's unyielding determination to assert his dominance.

Vasuki's eyes burned with determination, his resolve unwavering as he tapped into the full extent of his power. Cosmic energies surged through him, an intricate fusion of air and water that manifested as a radiant shield of light. As the massive vortex collided with the barrier, a dazzling explosion of light and energy erupted, illuminating the cosmic arena in a breathtaking spectacle.

The clash of the elements unfolded like a symphony, a perfect harmony of power and resilience—a dance that reverberated with the very heartbeat of the cosmos. The arena itself became a cauldron, simmering with creation and destruction, a living testament to the balance Vasuki was sworn to protect.

In a rare moment of clarity, Vasuki sensed the point of perfect harmony—the delicate balance where air and water could coexist in seamless unity. With focused intent, he redirected the energy of Varuna's tidal wave, guiding it with ease and transforming the fierce vortex into a radiant display of elemental beauty, a true testament to the power of balance.

As the ocean storm faded, the arena fell into quiet stillness, leaving Vasuki standing at its center—unscathed, his presence unwavering. The chaos of the waves had subsided, but his calm remained, a silent testament to his mastery. Varuna, watching this display of strength and balance, felt a deep sense of respect for his rival. With a nod, he acknowledged the power of harmony that had guided Vasuki's every move—recognizing that true strength lay in the delicate equilibrium between forces, not in their sheer might.

"You have calmed the waters, Vasuki," Varuna conceded, his voice a blend of admiration and acceptance. "The harmony of elements is a force to be reckoned with. But remember, the depths of the ocean are ever-changing, and the currents of the unknown are ever-present."

Varuna's words resonated with the depth of his understanding, carrying the quiet weight of wisdom. He recognized that the unknown, while a force of immense power, could only be navigated with balance and insight. In Vasuki, he saw a kindred spirit—a being who, like him, understood that harmony was the key to surviving the chaos that surrounded them.

As Varuna's form began to fade, dissolving into the vastness of the ether, Vasuki remained standing in the cosmic arena, lost in thought. The echoes of their encounter lingered in the air as he reflected on the lessons learned. The battle had tested his resolve, his understanding, and his mastery over the elements. But more than that, it had taught him that the dance of balance was never still—it was fluid, dynamic, and ever-evolving. It was a rhythm that shifted with time, a constant reminder that harmony was not a fixed state, but a living, breathing force.

The cosmic realm, with its infinite expanse, had revealed to Vasuki the profound importance of harmony in the face of conflict, the strength that could be found in equilibrium amidst chaos. As a guardian of balance, his role was both a heavy responsibility and an honored privilege—a reflection of the wisdom he had gathered through countless trials and the deep understanding he had forged over time.

But the cosmic arena shifted once again, its vastness glowing with an ethereal light as the elements rearranged themselves, signaling the arrival of Shiva—the destroyer and transformer. His presence was like a storm, a living embodiment of the endless cycle of creation and destruction. The ground trembled underfoot, and the skies darkened, as if the very cosmos bent to acknowledge the weight of his arrival.

Shiva emerged with an overwhelming aura, his skin the color of ash, a reflection of his eternal nature. His dreadlocked hair coiled around his neck like serpents, and his third eye—glowing with divine insight—shone with an intensity that seemed to pierce through time itself. He was the harbinger of both destruction and renewal, a force that transcended mortal understanding, stretching far beyond the limitations of time and space.

His eyes seemed to capture the essence of the infinite, holding within them the cycles of birth, death, and rebirth. Each glance seemed to encompass lifetimes, as though his very gaze could see the past, present, and future all at once. When he spoke, his voice rumbled like thunder, carrying with it a mix of challenge and curiosity, as though the universe itself was questioning and learning from his presence.

"Vasuki, keeper of the balance," Shiva intoned, his voice echoing across the cosmic expanse, "you stand at the crossroads of creation and destruction. Can you withstand the power of transformation?"

Vasuki stood poised, his serpentine form coiling gracefully against the celestial expanse. His scales shimmered with an ethereal glow, a mesmerizing display of colors that reflected the depth of his divine lineage. Despite the turmoil that stirred within him, he met Shiva's gaze with a calm, unwavering resolve. His presence radiated an inner strength, a quiet determination that spoke of a purpose unbroken by the forces around him. In that moment, he was not just a guardian of balance, but a symbol of resilience—a being whose spirit remained steadfast even in the face of the most profound challenges.

"The cycle of creation and destruction is indeed a force of transformation, Shiva," Vasuki replied, his voice smooth and unwavering. "But without balance, it becomes a force of chaos. It is the harmony of elements that allows creation to flourish and ensures the cosmos remains in equilibrium."

Shiva regarded Vasuki with a measured intensity, the flicker of a smile dancing across his lips. "Balance, Vasuki, is but a momentary state in the ever-changing dance of existence. Destruction is necessary for creation to thrive, and through transformation, the universe finds its true potential."

Shiva's presence was a living embodiment of the ultimate truth—that destruction was not an end but a vital precursor to renewal. He was the embodiment of the paradox that defines existence: life and death intertwined, where each ending held the potential for a new beginning. In his essence, there was no finality, only transformation—proof that from the ashes of destruction, new life would always rise. His very being whispered that in the cycles of creation and destruction, nothing was ever truly lost; it was all part of the eternal flow of existence.

Vasuki nodded, acknowledging Shiva's perspective. "True, Shiva, destruction paves the way for rebirth, but unchecked, it can lead to chaos and despair. Balance is not a static state; it is a dynamic harmony that sustains the cycle of existence."

Vasuki's conviction was born from a deep understanding—that true balance was not merely the absence of conflict, but the delicate art of maintaining harmony amidst opposing forces. It was a wisdom that transcended mere logic, rooted in the awareness that life itself was a constant dance between creation and destruction, light and dark.

As their philosophical dialogue deepened, the very air in the arena began to hum with palpable energy, a sign of the impending clash between titanic forces. The cosmos seemed to hold its breath, sensing that this battle would shape the fate of countless worlds, its outcome rippling through time and space.

Shiva extended his hand, and the universe responded as if it were alive—a symphony of energies swirling into motion. Forces collided around Vasuki, encircling him in a vortex of seething power, a cosmic storm that pulsed with the raw essence of transformation. The energies twisted and churned, an unruly entity of their own as if they were testing Vasuki's very resolve and his mastery over the forces he commanded.

The arena itself transformed into a crucible of energy and light, as Shiva unleashed his cosmic onslaught. His command over the elements was absolute, and the forces he wielded were a testament to his role as both the destroyer and the transformer. With each wave of energy, the very fabric of existence seemed to bend and shift, responding to his will as though the universe itself acknowledged his power.

Vasuki, however, remained undeterred. With unwavering focus, he met the challenge head-on, his form weaving through the swirling cosmic energies with a grace that seemed to transcend the chaos of the elements around him. Every movement was a dance of precision and purpose, each coil and twist a silent testament to his profound mastery over the forces of nature.

Drawing upon the grounding power of the earth, Vasuki summoned a barrier that rose steadily over the arena, anchoring the volatile energies and softening the cosmic fury. The earth responded in a surge of power, rising like clouds of dust, forming a shield of stability amid the storm. It stood as a symbol of balance—a quiet force of resistance against the maelstrom of creation and destruction that raged all around. Through it all, Vasuki remained calm in the eye of the storm, a reminder that even in the face of the most overwhelming forces, there is strength in steadiness and harmony.

Shiva's laughter echoed through the arena—a sound like rolling thunder—filled with admiration and challenge. "Impressive, serpent, but can you withstand the true fury of transformation?"

With a single, powerful gesture, Shiva summoned a force that spiraled toward Vasuki—a vortex of destruction, alive with raw energy, threatening to consume him entirely. The winds howled, and the energies roared, pulsing with an intensity all their own, driven by Shiva's indomitable will. It was a force that embodied the relentless cycle of life and death—the eternal flow of creation and destruction.

Vasuki's eyes shone with unwavering determination as he called upon the full depth of his power. Cosmic energies surged through him, a blend of earth and celestial forces, and manifested into a radiant shield that shimmered with a divine light. When the vortex of energy collided with the barrier, it sparked into a dazzling spectacle—a vibrant dance of light and energy that seemed to pulse with the very heartbeat of the cosmos.

The clash of elements was nothing short of a symphony—an intricate harmony of power and resilience, each force striving to assert itself while maintaining the balance Vasuki so fiercely protected. The arena itself became a cauldron, simmering with creation and destruction, where the elemental forces of the universe converged in a grand, cosmic tapestry.

In a moment of profound clarity, Vasuki sensed the point of perfect harmony—the delicate balance where earth and cosmic forces could coexist in seamless unity. With a focused will, he gently redirected Shiva's overwhelming energies, transforming the destructive vortex into a radiant display of elemental beauty, a harmonious fusion of fire, water, air, and earth.

As the cosmic storm gradually subsided, Vasuki remained standing amidst the stillness, untouched and unwavering. The tumultuous forces that had raged around him now lay quiet as if acknowledging his strength. His mastery over the elements was unmistakable, evident in the calm that followed the storm. It was a testament to his deep understanding of the delicate, intricate dance of balance—a wisdom that allowed him to navigate the most chaotic forces with grace and precision.

Shiva observed the serpent's triumph with a nod of respect—acknowledging Vasuki's strength and wisdom. "You have mastered the cycle, Vasuki," he conceded, his voice a blend of admiration and acceptance. "The harmony of elements is a force to be reckoned with. But remember, the cycle of creation and destruction is eternal, and the forces of transformation are ever-present."

His words resonated with the weight of deep understanding, a recognition that transformation was not just a singular event but an ongoing process that continually shaped the very fabric of reality. Each shift, each change, was part of a greater cycle, a flow of energy that could never truly be stopped.

As Shiva withdrew, his form slowly dissipating into the ether, Vasuki stood alone in the cosmic arena. The echoes of their divine conflict lingered in the air, a silent reminder of the power they had just wielded. The trials he had faced had tested him in ways he had never imagined—challenging his resolve, his understanding, and his control over the elements. But through each encounter, he had come to grasp the true nature of balance: not something static or easily maintained, but a delicate harmony that required constant care to sustain the universe itself.

The lessons of the divine council continued to resonate in his mind, each one a guide for the path that lay ahead. The cosmic realm, he now understood, was a reflection of the mortal world. Here, too, the struggle for balance played out in countless forms—whether through the forces of nature, the human spirit, or the intricate webs of fate. Vasuki's role as a guardian of harmony was not merely a duty; it was a privilege—a testament to the wisdom he had earned through his trials and to the unyielding responsibility he carried to protect the fragile equilibrium that sustained both realms.

As the cosmic arena slowly faded into the ether, Vasuki felt the undeniable pull of the mortal realm—an irresistible call to action that stirred deep within his soul. It was a reminder that his work was not yet done and that the challenges ahead would be immense, but he was no longer the same as he had been before. Armed with the lessons of the past and strengthened by the resolve of the present, he was ready to face whatever lay before him.

The cosmic balance, he knew, was eternal. It was an unbroken thread that wove through time and space, and as its guardian, Vasuki's duty was clear: to protect and uphold the harmony that sustained the very fabric of the universe. But he also understood that this path of balance was not merely a destination—it was a continuous journey, a living force that required constant vigilance and care.

In the ever-turning wheel of existence, Vasuki had come to realize his place. He was not just a spectator but a pivotal force in the dance of creation and destruction, a beacon of stability in a universe forever in flux. His role was both sacred and infinite—one that he would embrace with unwavering purpose, for as long as the cycle of balance endured.

Chapter 10: The Beginning of the End

The clock ticked slowly toward midnight, each second punctuated by the rhythmic click of gears echoing through the museum's grand hall. Outside, New York City pulsed with life, its streets alive with the hum of a city that never slept, completely unaware of the storm quietly gathering within one of its most cherished cultural landmarks. The city's vibrant energy, chaotic yet familiar, provided the perfect backdrop for a confrontation that would alter the course of worlds.

Inside the museum, the air was thick with a sense of anticipation. Shadows flickered across the stone walls, cast by the soft, almost mystical glow of ancient artifacts, which seemed to shimmer and breathe under the moonlight. This museum, more than a mere collection of relics, was a sanctuary—an untouched fortress where the past came alive, whispering the forgotten stories of gods and heroes who once walked among men.

In a room filled with shelves of weathered, leather-bound books and treasures from lost civilizations, Vikram and his team gathered around a large oak table. The space, usually a haven for academic debates and quiet discoveries, had been transformed into a war room, its air now thick with tension and purpose. The gravity of the moment was clear in every glance exchanged—this was no longer about knowledge or exploration; it was about survival, and the fate of the world hung in the balance.

Vikram stood at the head of the table, his gaze sweeping over his team. His eyes, sharp and unwavering, moved from face to face, a silent strength in his expression—a mix of determination and gratitude. In this room, he was more than just a vessel for Vasuki, the ancient serpent deity. He was a leader entrusted with the weighty responsibility of the fate of two worlds. The gravity of the task ahead weighed heavily on him, yet his resolve remained firm.

Beside him stood Maya, her presence a steadying force. She radiated strength and clarity, her dark hair cascading over her shoulders in waves. But it was the fire in her eyes that spoke volumes—an intensity that mirrored her unwavering commitment. She was more than just his partner in this battle; she was his confidante, the one who kept him grounded, reminding him of the humanity that remained even in the face of the unimaginable.

At the table's right, Anjali was absorbed in the task at hand, her fingers tracing the delicate lines of Sanskrit texts and digital maps spread before her. Her brow furrowed in concentration as she sifted through ancient manuscripts and modern data, her mind moving at lightning speed, a whirlwind of calculations and interpretations. Anjali's intellect was her greatest weapon, and she wielded it with unmatched precision. Her passion for the truth drove her to push through the challenges with a focused determination. Each of them brought something vital to the table, and together, they were the force that would determine the future.

Raj sat hunched over multiple monitors, his glasses reflecting the soft glow of the screens as he sifted through security footage and data streams. The museum's schematics flickered on one of the monitors, and his fingers danced across the keyboard, his mind moving just as fast. With his expertise in both ancient scripts and modern technology, he was an invaluable asset to the team, seamlessly bridging the gap between the long-forgotten past and the rapidly advancing present.

Beside him sat Rohan, ever the skeptic who had slowly transformed into a true believer. His fingers moved swiftly over the sleek laptop in front of him, orchestrating a network of surveillance drones that hovered just outside the museum, their infrared cameras silently scanning for any sign of danger. Rohan's technical prowess was matched only by the unwavering trust he now placed in the mission they had set before them. The cause had become more than just a task; it was something he now wholeheartedly believed in.

As the team settled into their roles, the room hummed with a charged energy. There was a palpable mix of anxiety and anticipation in the air, as if the weight of what lay ahead had already begun to settle on their shoulders. The scent of old books mingled with the whirring sound of high-tech equipment—a strange yet fitting juxtaposition that mirrored the collision of myth and science they were about to face. Everything felt like it was on the cusp of something monumental, and in that quiet yet intense moment, the team knew they were ready.

Vikram cleared his throat, drawing everyone's attention. "Tonight, we stand on the brink of something extraordinary," he began, his voice calm yet charged with emotion. "The Order of the Ecliptic will come for the artifact, and they will stop at nothing to obtain it. But we have something they don't—unity, knowledge, and the truth."

Maya added, her voice steady and filled with conviction, "We've prepared for this. Our bond is our strength, and our resolve will see us through. No matter what they throw at us, we will not falter."

Anjali looked up from her texts, her eyes filled with determination. "The prophecy speaks of a convergence—a choice that will shape the future. We have the power to protect the artifact and ensure that choice is made wisely."

Raj nodded, a reassuring smile on his lips. "I've reinforced the digital firewalls and encrypted all access points. The Order might be cunning, but they're not invincible. We'll be ready for them."

Rohan leaned back, his confidence apparent. "I've deployed the drones in a perimeter pattern. They'll alert us to any movement and give us a tactical advantage. If the Order thinks they can just walk in, they've got another thing coming."

Vikram felt a surge of pride and gratitude for his team. They had each taken on this challenge with courage and conviction, ready to face the unknown. "Remember," he said, "we're not just fighting for the artifact. We're fighting for the balance of the worlds and for the future of humanity."

In a secluded mansion nestled deep within the dense woods on the outskirts of the city, the Order of the Ecliptic gathered. The estate was a stunning fusion of old-world elegance and contemporary design, a place where time seemed to stand still. Its grand walls were adorned with rich tapestries, each one depicting celestial alignments and arcane symbols that whispered of forgotten knowledge. The air was thick with the weight of secrets, the hallways echoing with the faint murmur of voices that carried the forbidden truths of the ages.

At the head of the gathering sat Elder Matthias Richter, the Keeper of Secrets. His presence commanded the room with an undeniable force—an aura of authority mixed with an unsettling charisma. He was like a storm on the verge of breaking, his every movement deliberate and powerful. Matthias was a man who understood the nature of power—the intoxicating pull it had over others—and he wielded it with a cold ruthlessness that inspired both fear and unwavering loyalty in equal measure.

Around the long, polished table sat the Order's most formidable members. Each one brought a unique set of skills and insights that, together, made them a force to be reckoned with. The air was charged with purpose as they waited for the gathering to begin, knowing that their decisions here would set in motion events that could shape the future in unimaginable ways.

"In Shadows, We Illuminate."
"In Secrets, We Protect."

The Keeper addressed the council, his voice smooth yet commanding. "The artifact is the keystone to our ascension—a bridge between realms. We must secure it at any cost," he declared, his eyes scanning the room for any sign of dissent.

Lady Eleanor Blackwood nodded, her gaze fixed on the Keeper. "The artifact holds the power to unlock the secrets of the cosmos. We must not allow it to fall into the hands of those who lack the vision to wield it."

Sir Alistair Donovan leaned forward, his expression thoughtful. "Our operatives are in position. We have eyes inside the museum and agents ready to strike. The artifact will be ours before the night is over."

Madame Celeste DuBois' voice was a whisper, yet it carried an undeniable power. "I have foreseen this moment. The stars align in our favor, but we must be cautious. The artifact is protected by forces beyond our comprehension."

Contessa Isabella Rossi's lips curled into a knowing smile. "The city is our ally. I have ensured that distractions will keep the authorities occupied. Our path to the artifact will be unimpeded."

Hans Müller looked up from his screen, his voice confident. "I've implemented a cyber attack to disable the museum's security systems temporarily. We'll have a window of opportunity to make our move."

Dr. Naomi Sato finally spoke, her voice calm and measured. "I will lead the strike team. Vikram and his allies may prove formidable, but they are not invincible. We will neutralize any resistance."

The Keeper nodded, satisfied with the plan. "Then let us proceed. Tonight, we claim our destiny."

Back at the museum, the air was thick with anticipation. The team had prepared for this moment for what felt like an eternity, each member driven by a deep sense of duty and the unshakable awareness that the stakes had never been higher. What they were about to face would alter the course of their world—and possibly the world beyond.

In the artifact chamber, the atmosphere was charged with a palpable energy, almost as if the very walls of the room were holding their breath. At the center of it all, the artifact lay, a relic of immeasurable power and mystery. Its soft glow pulsed like a heartbeat, both a beacon of hope and a challenge that demanded to be understood. The artifact was an enigma, crafted with divine precision, its intricate symbols etched deep into the surface. These markings, glowing faintly, were remnants of an ancient script, their meanings long lost to time but still holding fragments of knowledge that had yet to be uncovered. Around it, the air hummed, vibrating with a subtle energy, as if the relic itself were alive—aware of the monumental weight of the moment.

Vikram stood before it, his figure silhouetted by the soft light of the artifact. The weight of responsibility pressed down on him, a dual burden that was both mortal and divine. In this moment, the two sides of his existence—his human identity and the divine essence of Vasuki—intertwined. He could feel the artifact resonate with him, as though acknowledging their shared fate. His gaze lingered on the symbols, tracing each line and curve, feeling the pull of ancient knowledge stir within him. The promise of power was undeniable, but so, too, was the understanding that this artifact was more than just an artifact. It was a guide, a beacon of balance and truth in a time when chaos threatened to overtake both worlds. It was the key, and Vikram knew that his next steps would determine not just his own future but the future of everything they had fought to protect.

Maya stepped forward, her presence a comforting anchor in the swirling uncertainty. She placed a gentle hand on Vikram's shoulder, her touch grounding him. Her eyes, deep and steady, searched his face for the answers they both sought. "Do you think we can trust the artifact to guide us?" Maya asked, her voice a blend of curiosity and resolve. Her question hung in the air, a testament to the doubts and hopes that lingered in her heart.

Vikram turned to her, his expression a reflection of his inner struggle. "The artifact is a beacon of balance and truth," he replied, his voice steady but carrying the weight of their shared burden. "It has guided us this far, and I believe it will continue to do so. But more importantly, we must trust in ourselves and the bonds we've forged. Together, we are stronger than any dark force."

Maya nodded, her faith in Vikram unwavering. "Then let's ensure those bonds hold," she said, her voice filled with determination.

Anjali, who had been silently studying the ancient texts scattered across the table, looked up, her eyes alight with revelation. She was the scholar of the group, her mind a treasury of languages and symbols that most would find incomprehensible. "I've deciphered more of the texts," she interjected, drawing the attention of the group. Her expression was a mix of curiosity and assurance, her excitement tempered by the gravity of their mission. "The prophecy speaks of a choice—a moment where paths converge, and destiny is decided. We are on the brink of that moment. It is said that those who stand at this crossroads must choose wisely, for their decision will echo through time."

Her words served as a sharp reminder of the monumental task that lay before them. Anjali's insights were more than just valuable—they were a lifeline, her knowledge a powerful weapon against the sea of uncertainties they faced. As she flipped through the pages of the leather-bound tome, her fingers moved gently over the delicate script, each touch a quiet reverence for the ancient wisdom contained within. She paused on a page, her brow furrowing in concentration, searching for the answers that could help them navigate the storm ahead. At that moment, her dedication was clear—every piece of knowledge she uncovered brought them one step closer to unraveling the mystery and taking control of their fate.

Raj approached his presence a steadying force amidst the tension. In his hands, he held a tablet, its screen flickering with streams of data. He was the bridge between the ancient and the modern, his expertise in technology and ancient scripts merging to create a formidable arsenal. "I've been monitoring the network," Raj said, his voice a calm, analytical counterpoint to the emotion-charged atmosphere. His eyes flicked between the tablet and the artifact, his mind a flurry of calculations and contingencies. "The Order is launching a cyber attack, but I've reinforced our defenses. They'll find no easy way in. Our digital fortifications are holding strong, but we must remain vigilant." His fingers danced over the screen, orchestrating a symphony of digital defenses designed to shield the museum from the Order's malevolent grasp. Raj's confidence was infectious—a testament to the countless hours he'd spent preparing for this very moment.

Rohan joined the group; his demeanor relaxed yet focused. Once a skeptic and now a believer, Rohan had become a vital part of their team; his technical expertise and growing faith in their mission were driving him forward. "The drones have picked up movement outside," Rohan reported, his gaze fixed on the live feeds streaming across his laptop screen. The drones, sleek and silent, hovered around the museum's perimeter, their infrared cameras scanning for any sign of intrusion. "The Order is making their move. We need to be ready." His words sent a ripple of adrenaline through the group, the reality of the impending confrontation sinking in. Rohan's fingers tapped commands into the keyboard, adjusting the drones' flight paths to maximize their coverage.

Vikram surveyed his team, a swell of pride and gratitude rising within him. They had come together from vastly different walks of life, each one brought to this moment by a deep sense of duty and the undeniable knowledge that the stakes were higher than ever. What stood before him now wasn't just a group of colleagues—they were a family, bound not by blood but by a shared purpose. Each of them brought something vital to the table, and together, they were united by a common belief: that, against all odds, they could change the course of history. In their eyes, Vikram saw the strength, resolve, and determination that made them more than just a team—they were a force, and the world would soon feel the impact of their actions.

"We've trained for this," Vikram said, his voice carrying the weight of leadership and the strength of unity. "The Order underestimates us, but they don't understand the power of our bond. We will face them with courage and conviction. We will protect the artifact and ensure that the balance of worlds is preserved."

His words echoed through the room, a rallying cry that cut through the tension and steeled their resolve. They felt a surge of determination, as though the very air around them had shifted. They were ready—ready to face the daunting challenges ahead, united in their mission to protect the artifact and fulfill the prophecy that had brought them all together.

The chamber fell silent again, the only sound the steady hum of energy emanating from the artifact, its power reverberating through the space. Each member of the team took a moment to reflect, their thoughts a swirling blend of hopes, fears, and the quiet, unwavering belief that they were on the right path. Despite the uncertainty ahead, there was a shared understanding among them that this was their destiny—one they had all chosen, one they had been prepared for.

As the minutes ticked by, the anticipation in the room became tangible, a force that seemed to press down on them from all sides. The weight of what lay ahead was heavy, but the conviction in their hearts remained unshaken. They were standing on the precipice of something greater than any of them could fully comprehend. Their choices and actions would shape not only their own futures but the future of both worlds. The responsibility was immense, but so was their strength. Together, they would face whatever came next.

Outside, the night deepened, the stars shimmering like distant beacons in the vast, endless sky. The city beyond continued in its usual rhythm, unaware of the storm that was about to break, of the ancient struggle that was soon to unfold in the heart of one of its cultural landmarks.

In the artifact chamber, Vikram and his team stood resolute, their hearts aligned with the singular purpose that had drawn them together. They had prepared for this moment, knowing the stakes and the weight of the responsibility they carried. Whatever lay ahead, they knew they would face it as one, each of them a vital part of the whole.

The clock struck midnight, and the museum seemed to exhale, holding its breath. Outside, New York City was cloaked in a rare silence; the usual hum of traffic and the energy of nightlife seemed to fade, as though the world itself sensed the tension building within the museum's walls. The moon hung high in the sky, its pale light casting long, eerie shadows across the museum's grand façade. Inside, the halls were bathed in a muted glow, the exhibits standing like silent sentinels in the dark, unaware of the battle that was about to erupt around them. In this stillness, the team gathered their strength, knowing that this moment, this confrontation, would change everything.

Vikram and his team stood in the artifact chamber, a place where time seemed to stand still, yet every moment was thick with tension. It was the very heart of their defense, the point where everything they'd worked for would either stand firm or crumble to dust. The chamber, with its soaring vaulted ceilings and walls adorned with ancient murals, was a curious mix of reverence and danger. It felt almost sacred, yet the air was charged with the weight of impending conflict.

At the center, on a stone pedestal, rested the artifact—an object of immense power. Its soft, otherworldly glow illuminated the room, stretching long shadows that danced across the walls as though alive. Those shadows seemed to pulse with their own secrets, watching, waiting, as if the artifact itself were aware of the darkness the Order of the Ecliptic sought to unleash.

Maya stood beside Vikram, her hand resting lightly on his arm. Her eyes were steady, filled with both determination and a quiet resolve that seemed to fortify the entire room. "We've prepared for this," she murmured, her voice barely above a whisper. "No matter what happens, we're not alone in this fight."

Vikram nodded, feeling the familiar weight of responsibility settle over him. "You're right," he replied, his gaze fixed on the artifact. "We're stronger together. The artifact chose us for a reason. We can't let the Order seize it."

Outside, the Order of the Ecliptic moved quietly, like a storm gathering its strength. Dr. Naomi Sato led the strike team, a presence that was both elegant and deadly. Every step she took was measured, every movement calculated. She was a master of control, her actions unfolding with a fluidity that betrayed the lethal precision beneath. Her dark eyes swept over the museum's perimeter, taking in every detail. She wasn't just observing—she was assessing, weighing the defenses with a mind sharpened by years of experience, always one step ahead, always prepared for what would come next.

"Remember your training," she whispered to her operatives, her voice as cold and sharp as a blade. "The artifact must be ours by night's end. No mistakes."

The operatives, dressed in sleek dark tactical gear, exchanged silent nods, a shared understanding passing between them. They were the Order's finest, each one a master in the art of stealth and combat. Moving as one, they flowed through the shadows, their movements so seamless they could have been part of the night itself.

A few steps behind, Lady Eleanor Blackwood walked with a calm, deliberate pace. While the others were fighters, she was a strategist, the mind behind the operation. Her presence spoke volumes about the operation's importance. In her hands, she cradled an ancient tome, its pages fragile and worn with age. The book seemed alive, its strange symbols and cryptic incantations radiating a quiet, unsettling power. It was more than just a relic—it was a key, one that pulsed with dark energy, carrying the weight of a history far older and more dangerous than anyone could imagine.

"We must act with precision," Eleanor whispered, her voice carrying an edge of excitement. "The artifact's power will soon be within our grasp. The balance of the world will shift in our favor."

Beside her, Hans Müller, the Order's technology and logistics expert, adjusted his headset, his fingers flying over a portable console. "I've overridden their external surveillance systems," he reported, his German accent clipped and efficient. "Our entry will be swift and undetected."

Sir Alistair Donovan surveyed the scene with a practiced eye. His role was to ensure that any countermeasures from the museum's defenders would be anticipated and neutralized. "Stay alert for surprises," he instructed his voice a low growl. "We cannot afford any interference."

Inside the artifact chamber, the air was thick with tension. Anjali sat at the control console, her eyes flicking between the screens that surrounded her—each one displaying complex schematics and real-time security feeds. She was in her element, a quiet force of focus amid the chaos. Her fingers moved swiftly over the keyboard, each keystroke purposeful, as if her thoughts were translating directly into action. Her mind was a whirlwind of calculations, interpreting data, and piecing together fragmented information, each moment bringing her closer to unlocking the secrets that could change everything.

"They're breaching the perimeter," Anjali announced, her voice calm but urgent. Her eyes flicked from screen to screen, analyzing the data with relentless focus. "We have maybe five minutes before they reach the inner corridors."

Raj, positioned nearby, tapped into the museum's mainframe with deft precision. His expertise in both technology and ancient scripts made him the linchpin of their digital defense. "I've rerouted the power grid to boost our defenses," he explained, his voice tinged with determination. "The electrified barriers should slow them down. They won't find easy passage."

He pushed his glasses up the bridge of his nose, the glow from the screens dancing off the lenses, casting sharp reflections on his focused face. His fingers flew over the keyboard, moving in a blur of motion as he fortified the digital defenses. With precision, he built firewalls and security loops, layering them one after another, each line of code a trap designed to catch any intruding signals. His concentration was unwavering, his mind completely absorbed in the virtual battlefield he was creating.

Rohan stood beside Raj, monitoring the drone feeds with intense concentration. The live feeds streamed across his laptop screen, displaying the movements of the Order's operatives as they advanced. "The Order's agents are converging on the artifact chamber," Rohan reported, his focus unwavering. "We've got incoming on all sides. They're using some kind of tech to jam our signals." His heart pounded with a mix of fear and adrenaline, the reality of the situation sinking in. But beneath the nerves was a steely resolve. He had come a long way from the skeptic he once was, now fully committed to the mission at hand.

Vikram felt a sudden surge of energy rush through him, a force that seemed to awaken something deep inside—something ancient, tied to his very nature. The connection to the artifact was immediate and intense, a blend of both familiarity and mystery. It was as though a forgotten power had stirred within him, now resonating with the artifact's pulse. He could feel their energies intertwining, a harmonious dance of light and shadow, as if they were two parts of a whole, bound by a force beyond time. It was an experience that both overwhelmed and grounded him, reminding him of a power he'd only begun to understand.

"We will not let them pass," Vikram declared, his voice a command that echoed through the chamber, infusing his team with a renewed sense of purpose. "Stand firm, and remember our purpose. The Order may be powerful, but they do not have what we possess—a bond forged in truth and shared destiny."

His words lingered in the air, charged with intensity—a call to action that solidified their resolve and drew them closer together in their mission.

Outside, the first wave of the Order's operatives moved swiftly toward the museum's entrance, their steps silent and deliberate. Dr. Naomi Sato, focused and unwavering, signaled for her team to advance. Her gaze never wavered from the target, and in her eyes was the certainty that they needed to strike quickly, using their numbers and the element of surprise to their advantage.

Inside, the museum's security systems hummed to life, lights flickering as Raj's rerouted energy surged through the circuits. One by one, the operatives breached the outer defenses, bypassing electronic locks and silencing alarms as though they'd done it a thousand times before. The mission was unfolding with flawless precision—an unstoppable force moving ever closer to its goal.

As they moved forward, a sudden crackle filled the air—the electrified barriers sprang to life, arcs of blue lightning dancing across their surfaces. The operatives faltered, momentarily thrown off by the unexpected obstacle. But Naomi remained calm, her focus unwavering. She didn't hesitate for a second. With a swift, authoritative gesture, she signaled two of her operatives. They moved quickly, pulling out specialized tools with practiced precision. Within moments, they began dismantling the barriers, their movements fluid and confident, as if they had anticipated the challenge all along. The team's momentum was unbroken, and they pressed on, undeterred.

Back in the artifact chamber, Anjali monitored their progress with a critical eye. "They're through the first layer of defenses," she reported, her fingers flying over the controls. "Activating secondary protocols now."

A sudden, deafening clang echoed through the corridors as reinforced steel doors slammed shut, sealing off every access point in their path. The intruders were momentarily trapped, forced to rethink their strategy and find another way through. But Anjali's sharp thinking gave them a brief reprieve. With a few swift commands, she managed to delay the systems, buying them precious moments. Her quick actions slowed the Order's advance, giving the team just enough time to regroup and reassess, their resolve strengthening in the face of the unexpected challenge.

Raj adjusted the security feeds, his gaze narrowing as he tracked the operatives' movements. "They're rerouting their paths," he said, his voice a mix of frustration and determination. "They're adapting faster than expected. We need to anticipate their next move."

Inside the museum, the Order's strike team moved with ruthless efficiency, each member executing their role with flawless precision. At the front stood Madame Celeste DuBois, the Order's enigmatic mystic. Her presence was both captivating and unsettling, an aura of darkness that seemed to warp the very air around her. With her eyes closed and her lips barely moving, she whispered ancient words, her incantations weaving an invisible shroud of illusion. The air thickened, and for those who might have been watching, the team seemed to vanish, swallowed up by the silence and shadows she conjured, their movements now hidden from prying eyes.

"The defenders rely too heavily on their machines," Celeste murmured, her voice a soft chant that carried through the corridors. "Let us see how they fare against the unseen."

A veil of shadow flowed from Madame Celeste DuBois' fingertips, swirling around her team like a living thing, wrapping them in a cloak of darkness so thick it seemed impenetrable. With the shadows as their ally, they moved like phantoms, their forms melting into the darkness of the museum's halls, undetected by anyone who might have been watching.

Meanwhile, Contessa Isabella Rossi, the Order's political strategist and expert in influence, observed the scene with a calculating gaze. Combat was not her battlefield; her strength lay in maneuvering the levers of power from behind the scenes. Calmly, she accessed her network, pulling strings in the shadows—manipulating local authorities and media outlets to stir chaos, creating distractions that would keep the public's attention elsewhere, and ensuring the Order's plan could unfold without a hitch.

"The museum's defenders are resourceful, but they cannot withstand a coordinated assault," Isabella noted, her voice a confident lilt that belied the danger of their mission. "We must keep them occupied while our operatives secure the artifact."

Sir Alistair Donovan, the mastermind behind the Order's intelligence operations, stood at the heart of their strategy, his mind weaving a web of calculated moves and countermeasures. His voice was cold and measured as he delivered his report. "We've intercepted their communications," he said, his tone devoid of emotion. "Their plans are clever but predictable. Deploy the backup team to the eastern wing. We'll hit them from two fronts and overwhelm their defenses." His words were precise, each one a command that shaped the next phase of their assault.

Meanwhile, back in the artifact chamber, Vikram and his team steeled themselves for what they knew was coming. They had fortified their position, making use of every resource at their disposal, knowing they would need every advantage to hold off the Order's relentless pursuit. The silence around them was heavy, charged with anticipation, as they prepared for the confrontation that could decide everything.

Maya adjusted her earpiece, maintaining a constant line of communication with her teammates. "Stay alert, everyone. We can't afford any slip-ups," she said, her voice a steady reminder of the stakes they faced. "Remember, the artifact is our priority. Keep it safe at all costs."

Anjali continued to scan the digital interface, her mind racing to decode any potential weaknesses in the Order's strategy. "If we can identify their command structure, we might be able to disrupt their coordination," she suggested, her eyes alight with possibility.

Raj nodded, already working to hack into the Order's communications network. "I'm on it," he replied, his fingers flying over the keyboard as he attempted to break through their encrypted channels. "If we can isolate their signals, we can feed them false data and slow their advance."

Rohan kept his focus on the drone feeds, the flickering images revealing the Order's movements as they pressed deeper into the museum. "They're splitting into smaller teams," he observed, his voice a mix of concern and determination. "We need to adapt our strategy to counter their tactics."

Vikram stood in the center of the room, a quiet tension hanging in the air around him. The weight of his responsibilities pressed down on him—he was both the leader guiding his team and the protector of something far greater than himself. He could feel the artifact's energy pulse through him, its power thrumming in his veins, reminding him of the divine force that lay within him. He closed his eyes for a moment, inhaling deeply to steady his racing thoughts. As the room seemed to hold its breath with him, he centered himself, preparing for the challenge that awaited.

"We've trained for this," Vikram reminded his team, his voice resonating with calm authority. "The Order may be skilled, but they underestimate the strength of our conviction. We will defend the artifact and preserve the balance of the worlds."

His words rang out in the chamber, each syllable sharp and resolute, a rallying cry that seemed to solidify their resolve and bind them together in a shared purpose. The team exchanged knowing nods, their determination unshakable as they readied themselves for the battle that was closing in on them.

Outside, the Order's operatives moved with quiet efficiency, their every step calculated and deliberate. They infiltrated the inner corridors, their figures barely visible in the low light. The dim glow of emergency lights flickered overhead, casting long, eerie shadows across the polished floors as they advanced without hesitation, their presence nearly undetectable in the silence that enveloped the museum.

His words rang out in the chamber, each syllable sharp and resolute, a rallying cry that seemed to solidify their resolve and bind them together in a shared purpose. The team exchanged knowing nods, their determination unshakable as they readied themselves for the battle that was closing in on them.

Outside, the Order's operatives moved with quiet efficiency, their every step calculated and deliberate. They infiltrated the inner corridors, their figures barely visible in the low light. The dim glow of emergency lights flickered overhead, casting long, eerie shadows across the polished floors as they advanced without hesitation, their presence nearly undetectable in the silence that enveloped the museum.

"They're almost here," she warned, her voice steady despite the urgency of the situation. "Get ready."

The moment had finally come. Vikram stepped to the front, his presence steady and unwavering. The energy of the artifact surged through him, a living force that pulsed in tune with his very being. He could feel it deep within, an undeniable echo of his true nature as Vasuki, the divine serpent king, awakening in the depths of his soul.

With a heavy creak, the doors to the artifact chamber swung open, and the Order's operatives poured in, a wave of darkness that swept through the room with deadly precision. Their intent was clear: ruthless, unstoppable, and focused entirely on their goal. Vikram stood firm, the weight of his divine power grounding him as the battle for the artifact began.

Maya stepped forward, her eyes blazing with determination. "You won't take the artifact," she declared, her voice unwavering as she faced their adversaries. "This ends here."

Chapter 11: Convergence

The artifact chamber stretched before her like a maze, its stone walls steeped in history, shadows flickering like ghosts from another time. The air hummed with a charged energy, thick with both expectation and something darker—an ancient power that whispered through the stones. Naomi Sato stood at the threshold, her gaze fixed on Maya Singh. Her eyes glinted with a predatory satisfaction as if every step had led to this moment. There was a quiet confidence in the way she regarded Maya, the weight of the chamber and its secrets pressing down on both of them.

"Brave words," Naomi said, her voice laced with a venomous edge. "But bravery alone won't save you."

Maya's gaze was unwavering, her stance radiating defiant strength. "Nor will your arrogance," she shot back, her voice a steady counterpoint to the chaos that was about to unfold.

Naomi's taunting words lingered in the air like a challenge, and in an instant, the room erupted into motion. The Order's operatives surged forward, their dark figures cutting through the dim light, stark against the shimmering glow of the artifact. The tension in the air thickened, crackling with the promise of conflict, as Vikram's team braced themselves. Every member was poised, their resolve unshakable, ready to face the storm that was about to break. The chamber itself seemed to hold its breath, caught in a fragile moment of stillness, as if it, too, knew that chaos was only a heartbeat away.

Dr. Vikram Nair, though he appeared the picture of a scholar, carried within him the essence of something far older, a power that pulsed through his very being. At this moment, his hidden divine nature stirred within, like the restless presence of an ancient serpent deity. It flowed through his veins, sharpening his senses and lending him a fluid grace and speed that defied his appearance. He moved effortlessly through the chamber, a shadow weaving through the chaos, each step deliberate, each motion part of a dance perfected by purpose. His hands, calm and unwavering, deflected a barrage of strikes with an ease that seemed almost otherworldly, responding with precise counters that struck with devastating force. His eyes gleamed with a serpentine glint as he parried and retaliated, each move a fusion of power and precision. The artifact's influence pulsed within him, guiding his strikes with an instinctive clarity that went beyond mere technique. Ancient whispers filled his mind, stirring memories of long-forgotten power, reminding him of what he had once been.

As an operative lunged at him, dagger raised and gleaming, Vikram moved with a fluidity that seemed almost unnatural.

With a serpentine twist, he sidestepped the strike, his body reacting before his mind could even process the danger. The artifact's energy surged within him, sharpening his senses to a level that felt otherworldly. In one smooth motion, he spun, his arm cutting through the air in a graceful arc. His counterattack was swift and decisive, sending the assailant crashing to the stone floor with a force that seemed to come from somewhere beyond mortal strength. A brief flicker of ancient power glinted in his eyes, a silent reminder of the deity that slumbered within him, its presence flickering to life in the heat of the moment.

In the heat of battle, Vikram's thoughts drifted back to the teachings of his youth when his father, a man of great wisdom, taught him the balance between knowledge and action. "Remember, Vikram," his father's voice echoed in his mind, "true strength lies in knowing when to wield your power and when to show restraint."

The memory anchored him, a steady force that reminded him of his true purpose—not just to fight, but to protect and preserve the knowledge and wisdom that the artifact held. The chaos of the room swirled around him, a blur of motion and noise, but Vikram's focus remained sharp, unwavering. Every movement, every breath, was in service to something greater.

Beside him, Maya Singh and Anjali Kapoor fought with seamless fluidity, their partnership honed by years of trust and shared experience. Maya's eyes, dark and intense, never wavered as she tracked her opponents, her gaze locked on each one with unrelenting focus. Her body moved with lethal grace, a blur of calculated action, as she carved her way through the enemy ranks like a storm. Each strike was a perfect blend of intellect and strength, her blade cutting through the air with a sharp, whistling song that echoed with precision and purpose.

Anjali, in the midst of the chaos, stood as an unmovable pillar. Her deep understanding of ancient symbols came to life in the form of glowing wards, their light flickering like fragile stars in the dim chamber. Each ward shimmered with a soft, radiant glow, forming an invisible barrier that absorbed the impact of every incoming attack. The strikes met her shield with quiet resistance, their force dissipating harmlessly into the air. As she chanted softly, the ancient words rolled from her lips in forgotten tongues, resonating with an otherworldly power. It was a deep, primal energy—mystical and profound—that seemed to echo through the very stone of the chamber, an unspoken promise of protection and strength.

"Anjali!" Maya called over the cacophony, her voice a beacon in the chaos. "The wards are holding, but we need to push forward!"

Anjali nodded, her eyes meeting Maya's with steely determination. "On your lead!" she replied, weaving another layer of protection around them. The glow of her wards cast a warm, protective light, their energy a bastion against the encroaching darkness.

Together, they advanced, an unstoppable blend of intellect and strength that no force could sway. Anjali's wards pulsed brighter with each chant, their luminous patterns dancing across the chamber walls, casting ever-changing shadows that seemed to move with a life of their own. Maya fought beside her, her every strike precise and calculated, a dance of raw power that sent adversaries falling in her wake, one after another.

Across the battlefield, Raj Mehta and Rohan Patel worked in perfect synchronization, using their technological ingenuity to outwit the Order's operatives. Raj unleashed a flurry of holographic decoys, their flickering images springing to life in a disorienting blur. The decoys moved with an eerie fluidity, a chaotic ballet of shifting figures that kept the enemy off balance. It was a dizzying spectacle, one that made it nearly impossible for the operatives to tell where reality ended and illusion began.

"Keep them guessing, Raj!" Rohan shouted, his fingers flying over the controls of a sleek tablet. His command of technology was masterful, orchestrating a symphony of noise and light that disoriented and distracted their foes.

Rohan, always the tech genius, commanded a swarm of drones that hovered above like a metallic cloud. The buzz of their engines filled the air, a constant hum that was both unsettling and purposeful. Each drone emitted rapid flashes of light and high-pitched sounds that sliced through the chaos below, throwing the enemy's formations into disarray. The drones darted and weaved with precision, releasing clouds of smoke and blinding bursts of light that turned the chamber into a dizzying kaleidoscope of shifting shadows and confusion. Every move was calculated, a brilliant disruption that left the operatives struggling to regain their bearings.

"Deploying smokescreen," Rohan announced, his voice steady amidst the chaos. With a swift swipe on his tablet, he released a plume of dense smoke that enveloped the chamber, creating a cover that further disoriented their adversaries.

Raj grinned, his eyes gleaming with mischievous excitement. "Let's give them a show they won't forget!" With a series of deft movements, he activated a new sequence of holograms that depicted a fearsome beast—a creature from ancient myth that seemed to rise from the smoke itself. The operatives faltered, their fear palpable as they hesitated, uncertain of what was real and what was illusion.

Amid the whirlwind of chaos, Raj and Rohan shared a fleeting glance, a quiet acknowledgment that passed between them without a word. It was a glance that spoke volumes, revealing the depth of their understanding and the bond they had forged over years of friendship and trust. They had prepared for this moment together, anticipating every detail. Each hologram they projected was a carefully crafted illusion, each drone's movement a deliberate step in a much larger strategy. It wasn't just the technology they wielded—it was a symphony of calculated decisions, the result of a partnership built on mutual respect and an unspoken commitment to each other's success.

Despite the overwhelming numbers of the Order, Vikram's team stood firm, their resolve unwavering. The power of the artifact surged through them, its radiant energy infusing them with a strength that felt almost otherworldly, a beacon of light pushing back against the looming darkness. Each team member fought not just with skill but with a deep sense of purpose, their movements driven by the weight of their mission. Together, they formed an unbreakable line, their efforts seamlessly blending into a powerful force. Every strike, every block, every counterattack was a testament to their shared commitment to protect the artifact and the ancient secrets it held—no matter the cost.

The chamber had become a maelstrom of clashing forces—a cacophony of power and chaos that shook the very stone around them. Yet, within the storm, Vikram's team moved with an unspoken precision, each action flowing seamlessly into the next. Their coordination was a reflection of years of trust and unity, their movements a blend of strategy and strength that kept the enemy at bay.

Vikram felt the artifact's power surge through him, its energy both familiar and comforting, like an old friend awakening within him. It was as though the artifact sensed his divine nature, amplifying his abilities and blurring the line between human skill and something greater. With a fluid motion, he parried another strike, the ease with which he deflected it almost unnatural. In the next breath, his counterattack was swift and decisive, his movements guided by something far beyond the mortal realm.

"Keep pushing!" Vikram urged, his voice rising above the clamor of battle. "We're turning the tide!"

Maya nodded, her eyes fierce with determination. "They're faltering," she called out, her voice a rallying cry for her teammates. "We can do this!"

Anjali's wards continued to glow, their light a shield against the enemy's relentless onslaught. "Stand firm!" she intoned her voice a steady beacon of calm amidst the storm. Her chants, infused with the power of ancient languages, resonated with a force that was both protective and empowering.

Raj and Rohan held their technological edge with unyielding determination, their every move a calculated barrage of decoys and distractions. The air around them seemed to bend at their will, smoke swirling and flashes of blinding light erupting in rapid succession, each burst a carefully crafted disruption that kept the enemy scrambling, never able to find their footing.

Amid the chaos, Vikram stood firm, a pillar of strength and unwavering resolve. The artifact's steady pulse resonated in the air, its glow a constant reminder of the purpose they shared and the unity that bound them together. The energy that surged through him was both ancient and enduring, a powerful echo of the divine heritage that lived within him, reminding him with each breath that he was not just fighting for survival but for something much greater than himself.

In the heart of the battle, the artifact began to pulse, its glow intensifying with each passing moment, building to a blinding crescendo. For a brief, suspended moment, the operatives of the Order faltered, their eyes fixed on the radiant display before them. The air seemed to hum with anticipation—this was the moment the artifact would act. With a sudden, explosive surge, it released a wave of energy that swept across the chamber like an unstoppable tidal force.

The energy coursed through Vikram and his team, revitalizing them and filling their bodies with renewed strength and purpose. Every movement became sharper, every action more decisive. To their enemies, however, the wave was chaos incarnate. It struck them with such force that they were thrown off balance, struggling to recover as the relentless power of the artifact tore through their ranks. It was a moment of divine intervention, and the tide of battle had irrevocably shifted.

Vikram seized the moment, charging forward with a newfound intensity. The artifact's power flowed through him like wildfire, sharpening his senses and giving his strikes an unstoppable force. He moved with the swiftness of a storm, his every motion a blur of divine precision, leaving a trail of incapacitated foes in his wake. Each step seemed to echo with the weight of ancient power, and his enemies could do little but fall before him.

Maya and Anjali were right behind him, their movements fueled by the same surge of energy. Their attacks became almost otherworldly, each strike sharper, faster, and more precise. With unwavering resolve, they dismantled the remaining operatives, their every action a testament to the strength of their unity. The artifact's energy swirled around them, an invisible force that created a protective barrier, pushing back anyone who dared to approach. Together, they were an unstoppable force, a perfect storm of power and purpose.

Raj and Rohan, emboldened by the artifact's surge of power, pushed forward with renewed intensity. Raj's decoys became even more lifelike, each illusion so convincing that it was nearly impossible to tell them from reality. Rohan's drones moved with an almost eerie synchronization, their fluid motions giving the impression of sentience as they outmaneuvered the enemy with precision. Together, their technological mastery reshaped the battlefield, a testament to human ingenuity, determination, and the perfect marriage of mind and machine.

As the battle unfolded, the Order's operatives began to crumble under the relentless pressure. Their once-solid resolve wavered in the face of Vikram's unyielding defense. What had started as a fierce assault now turned into a chaotic retreat, the operatives pulling back with a mix of frustration and defeat. The tide of battle had shifted irreversibly, and Vikram's team pressed their advantage, moving with a singular focus and renewed vigor, determined to finish what they had started.

Naomi, sensing the fragility of their position, gave a sharp signal for retreat. Her operatives responded instantly, moving with the precision of well-trained soldiers, their steps swift and silent as they vanished into the shadows. The chamber, which had been a tumult of clashing wills just moments before, now stood still—its walls a silent witness to the fierce battle that had unfolded within.

As the dust began to settle and the echoes of combat faded into a heavy silence, Vikram's team stood tall, their unity and unwavering resolve having carried them through. The chamber, once a battleground, now felt like a sanctuary, its sacred space preserved and protected against the encroaching darkness that had threatened to overrun it. The victory was theirs, not just in the fight but in the strength of their collective spirit.

Vikram took a slow, measured breath, surveying the aftermath with a deep sense of relief and accomplishment. The artifact was secure, its glow steady and reassuring, a beacon of hope amidst the chaos. He felt a swell of pride in his chest as he looked at his team, their faces marked by the weariness of battle but also the quiet satisfaction that came with a hard-won victory. They had done it—they had defended the artifact, fending off the Order's relentless attempts to seize its power.

But as he stood there, a quiet understanding settled over him. This victory, though significant, was just the beginning. The artifact held mysteries far beyond their grasp, and the shadow of the Order still loomed, its threat far from vanquished. The road ahead was uncertain, but one thing was clear: their fight was far from over. And together, they would face whatever came next.

"We did it," Maya said, her voice a mixture of awe and gratitude. Her gaze swept over the chamber, taking in the aftermath of their triumph. "We protected the artifact."

Anjali nodded her expression a blend of exhaustion and triumph. "It wasn't easy," she acknowledged, her voice filled with the weight of their achievement. "But we held our ground. The Order won't give up easily, but neither will we."

Raj and Rohan exchanged a glance, their expressions a mix of fatigue and determination. "We may have won this battle," Raj remarked, his voice a steady reminder of the ongoing struggle, "but the war is far from over."

Rohan nodded in agreement, his mind already turning to the challenges that lay ahead. "We'll be ready for whatever comes next," he assured them, his voice a promise of future resolve.

As the team regrouped, readying themselves for the challenges to come, Vikram felt a quiet surge of purpose. The battle had pushed them to their limits, but it had also deepened their bond and fortified their resolve. The artifact, glowing softly in the dim light, stood as a silent reminder of their victory—a symbol of hope and power in the face of uncertainty.

"We have much to learn from this experience," Vikram acknowledged, his gaze sweeping over his team with a sense of pride and gratitude. "But we also have much to be thankful for. Together, we are a force to be reckoned with."

As the chamber fell into silence, a figure slowly emerged from the shadows—the Keeper of Secrets, Elder Matthias Richter. His eyes, sharp and calculating, scanned the scene with a mixture of curiosity and something more elusive, a hidden intent that seemed to hang in the air. He moved toward Vikram with a quiet authority, his presence both commanding and shrouded in mystery, as if every step he took carried weight and purpose.

The Keeper nodded slowly, his voice a resonant baritone that carried both wisdom and challenge. "You have done well to protect the artifact, Dr. Nair. You've proven to be quite a formidable opponent. It is no small feat to repel the forces of the Order so effectively. Truly, the artifact has chosen its guardian well," he acknowledged, his gaze steady and appraising. "But this is far from over."

Vikram locked eyes with the Keeper, his gaze steady and resolute. The adrenaline of battle still buzzed in his veins, but he watched the Keeper warily, sensing something more in his presence. The hum of the artifact's energy lingered within him, a reminder of the struggle they had just endured—and the ancient power that still eluded his full understanding. There was something strangely familiar in the Keeper's eyes, a recognition that unsettled Vikram, sending a subtle shiver down his spine. It was as if the Keeper saw something hidden within him—something Vikram himself hadn't fully grasped yet. The feeling grew stronger with each passing second, as though the Keeper knew more than he was willing to reveal.

"The Order's ambitions are relentless," the Keeper continued, his voice carrying an undercurrent of warning. "They will not rest until they have claimed the power they believe is rightfully theirs. The artifact is but one piece of a much larger puzzle."

Vikram nodded, his mind racing with possibilities. He could feel the weight of the Keeper's words, the gravity of the situation pressing upon him. "The artifact doesn't belong to the Order," Vikram said, his voice steady but laced with a hint of the uncertainty that churned beneath his calm exterior. "Nor does it belong to anyone seeking to exploit it for their own ends. We will continue to protect the artifact and uncover its secrets," he replied, his voice firm and determined.

The Keeper nodded slowly, his expression one of feigned sympathy. "Of course, of course. And yet, you must understand, the Order seeks only to harness the artifact's potential for a greater cause—a cause that transcends individual desires and ambitions."

Vikram narrowed his eyes, his skepticism plain. "And what cause is that, exactly? Power? Domination? The Order speaks of unity, but all I've seen is destruction and chaos in your wake."

The Keeper chuckled—a low, throaty sound that carried both amusement and condescension. "Ah, you misunderstand us, my dear Vasuki. The Order seeks knowledge and enlightenment—a path to bridging the ancient with the modern, the mythical with the scientific. With the artifact, we could achieve wonders beyond the comprehension of the ordinary mind."

Vikram's breath caught in his throat, his heart skipping a beat as the Keeper spoke his hidden identity. He had always felt there was something dormant inside him, a force beyond human understanding. But hearing it spoken aloud—being called *Vasuki,* the ancient serpent deity—was both exhilarating and unnerving. The weight of the words hung in the air, a truth he had long suspected but never fully embraced, and now it was out in the open, both a revelation and a burden.

"How do you know?" Vikram asked, his voice a mix of curiosity and caution.

The Keeper smiled faintly, his expression inscrutable. "I am the Keeper of Secrets, after all," he replied enigmatically. "I know much that others do not. Your journey has only just begun."

"The path you offer is a dangerous one," Vikram replied, his tone firm and unwavering. "It's a path that leads to destruction, not enlightenment. The artifact's power is not meant to be wielded by those who seek to dominate and control."

The Keeper's expression shifted subtly, a hint of frustration creeping into his otherwise composed demeanor. "Do you truly believe that you alone can safeguard the artifact's secrets? That you, with your mortal limitations, can stand against the forces that seek to unravel the very fabric of our reality?"

Vikram held the Keeper's gaze, his resolve unyielding. "I'm not alone. I have my team, and together, we've proven that we can stand against the Order. We protect the artifact not for power but to ensure it remains a beacon of hope and balance."

The Keeper's eyes glinted with a sharp, calculating light. "Hope and balance, you say?" he mused, his voice dropping to a conspiratorial whisper. "Consider this, Vasuki: With the Order, you could achieve so much more. Your divine heritage gives you the potential to reshape the world to bring about an era of unprecedented harmony. Think of the possibilities—what you could accomplish with our guidance."

For a brief moment, Vikram felt the pull of temptation. The thought of unlocking the full extent of his powers, of unraveling the vast mysteries hidden within him, was undeniably tempting. But as his gaze shifted to his team—Maya, Anjali, Raj, and Rohan—he was reminded of what truly mattered. The bonds they had built, the trust that ran deep between them, and the ideals they fought to protect. In that instant, the allure of power was overshadowed by the strength of their unity and the purpose they shared.

"No," Vikram said firmly, his voice carrying the weight of his conviction. "I won't be swayed by promises of power and glory. I know who I am, and I choose to stand with those who believe in a better future—one where knowledge is shared, not hoarded; where power is used to uplift, not oppress."

The Keeper's expression hardened, his eyes narrowing to slits as he realized his words had fallen on deaf ears. "You are a fool, Vasuki," he spat, his voice laced with disdain. "You have the power of a god, yet you choose to remain shackled by mortal ideals. But know this: The Order will not rest until the artifact is ours, and neither will I."

Vikram stepped forward, his stance unwavering. "You may try, Keeper, but we will be ready. The artifact chose me for a reason, and I will not let it fall into the hands of those who would misuse it."

The Keeper's gaze lingered on Vikram for a moment longer, a mixture of frustration and grudging respect flickering in his eyes. "Very well," he said finally, his tone resigned yet steely. "But mark my words, Vasuki—the battle is far from over. The Order will return, and when we do, we will be stronger and more determined than ever."

With that, the Keeper turned sharply, his figure melting into the shadows as he disappeared. Vikram watched him vanish, a storm of emotions churning inside him. He had confronted the Keeper of Secrets and stood firm, his resolve unbroken, but the knowledge that the Order would not give up lingered heavily in his mind.

As the last echoes of the Keeper's departure faded into the stillness, Vikram turned to face his team. Their expressions were a mix of relief and unwavering determination. They had survived the battle, but he knew the path ahead would be filled with even greater challenges. Together, they had faced the storm—now, they would have to face whatever came next.

His words lingered in the air, resonating deeply with the team. Their unity, forged in the fires of battle, was a powerful reminder of their shared mission. They had faced the Order of the Ecliptic and emerged victorious, their bond unshaken in the face of overwhelming adversity. The battle was over, but the journey was far from finished.

As they stood together, side by side, their purpose and resolve unbreakable, the artifact's glow bathed the chamber in soft warmth. It was a light that carried with it the promise of hope, a beacon for the uncertain future that lay ahead. The path was unclear, but with the artifact safe and their spirits bolstered by the victory they had fought so hard to achieve,

Vikram and his team were ready. Their resolve was steadfast, their spirits unyielding, and their bond stronger than ever. Together, they would face whatever challenges awaited them.

The battle was over, but the true fight for the future had only just begun. With the power of the artifact and the spirit of Vasuki now within him, Vikram was ready to embrace his destiny. He understood the weight of what lay ahead—challenges that would test him in ways he could scarcely imagine.

The ancient artifact chamber, once a place of violent struggle, was now bathed in the soft, fading light of dawn. The chaos had given way to an unexpected serenity, the oppressive tension of conflict replaced by a quiet stillness. It was a silence that held the echoes of victory but also the weight of the cost they had paid.

Standing amidst the wreckage, Vikram Nair, a man who had long walked the line between his mortal self and his divine heritage, reflected on the journey that had brought him to this point. The path ahead was uncertain, but at that moment, he knew he was no longer the same man who had entered the chamber. The journey was far from over, and the future was his to shape.

Vikram's gaze was drawn to the artifact, now resting quietly in its protective casing. Its once-bright, pulsing glow had softened, now radiating a gentle light, as if it, too, recognized the end of a long, tumultuous journey. Taking a deep breath, Vikram felt the weight of his dual existence settles around him. It was a strange sensation—both lighter and heavier at the same time. The battle was over, but the lessons learned and the responsibilities that lay ahead were only just beginning to unfold before him.

As he stood there, lost in thought, Maya Singh approached him. The soft glow of the artifact bathed her face, casting shadows that seemed to mirror the complexity of her own emotions. Her expression was a quiet mixture of relief and something deeper—unspoken yet understood. Her eyes met his, reflecting all the shared trials and victories they had faced together. Without a word, she reached out, her hand gently resting on his arm, a simple gesture that spoke volumes of their bond and everything they had endured.

"We did it," Maya said, her voice carrying a note of both triumph and tenderness. "But I can't help but wonder what comes next."

Vikram turned to her, his gaze meeting hers with profound intensity. "The battle was only a part of our journey, Maya. We've safeguarded the artifact, but the world is still full of challenges and mysteries. Our path is far from over."

Maya nodded, her eyes shining with a mixture of determination and affection. "Together, we've faced incredible odds. We've proven that we can overcome anything as long as we stand united."

As the team gathered, each member carried the weight of their shared struggles and victories. Anjali Kapoor, her practical field clothes now stained from the battle, walked over with a thoughtful look on her face.

"The wards and protections we relied upon were crucial," Anjali said, her voice steady. "But there are still forces out there that seek to disrupt the balance. We need to remain vigilant and continue our research."

Raj Mehta, his usual calm demeanor slightly marred by exhaustion, added, "The technological advancements we've made are significant, but we must keep evolving. The Order won't be the last threat we face."

Rohan Patel, ever the tech enthusiast, was busy analyzing data and recalibrating his equipment. "Our tech held up well, but we need to stay ahead. I'll start working on upgrades immediately."

Vikram looked around at his team, a sense of deep gratitude and pride filling his heart. "Your bravery, intelligence, and commitment have been extraordinary. This victory is just the beginning of a much larger journey."

The team paused for a moment of silence, each person lost in their thoughts about their journey and what lay ahead. The weight of their recent challenges lingered, but there was also a sense of hope for the new beginnings on the horizon.

Epilogue: The Promises of the Future

The city of New York spread out beneath a blanket of stars, its lively streets pulsing with energy and ambition. Far above the bustle, in a sleek penthouse overlooking Central Park, Aditya Varun stood like a quiet observer, reflecting on the recent chaos that had stirred beneath the city's hidden mystical currents.

The penthouse was a marvel of modern design, with expansive glass walls and polished marble floors offering sweeping views of the city below. Art from various cultures decorated the space, showcasing Aditya's deep appreciation for history and beauty—a refined taste honed over many lifetimes.

Aditya Varun, a formidable business tycoon and the reincarnation of Varuna, controlled vast water resources across the globe. His influence reached continents, spanning luxury resorts and cutting-edge innovations in water management. With each life he lived, his relentless pursuit of power and knowledge left its mark.

Tonight, Aditya wasn't alone. He had invited Cassandra Valois, a respected French expert in occult studies, to discuss the shifting balance of power that had caught his attention. The recent events surrounding the artifact—at the center of a fierce battle between ancient forces and those sworn to protect its secrets—had intrigued him in ways he hadn't expected.

The soft chime of the elevator signaled Cassandra's arrival, and Aditya turned away from the window, a glass of cognac in hand. Cassandra stepped in with her signature grace, her long dark hair flowing over her shoulders and her eyes gleaming with curiosity.

"Aditya," Cassandra greeted, her voice a melodic blend of French sophistication and academic authority. "Your penthouse is as impressive as always."

Aditya smiled, gesturing for her to join him in the sitting area, where a fire crackled softly, casting a warm glow over the room. "Thank you, Cassandra. Please make yourself comfortable. Would you like a drink?"

"Perhaps a glass of that exquisite red wine you keep hidden," she replied with a knowing smile.

Aditya chuckled quietly as he pulled a bottle of vintage Bordeaux from a hidden cabinet. As he poured the wine, his mind wandered to the nature of their conversation—a careful balance of mutual ambitions and unspoken agendas.

Once seated, Cassandra took a sip of her wine, her gaze fixed on Aditya with a mixture of respect and intrigue. "I understand you've been observing the recent events concerning the artifact. What are your thoughts on the matter?"

Aditya leaned back, his expression thoughtful yet controlled. "The artifact is a nexus of power, a relic of profound significance. Those who seek to control it and those who protect it are playing a game of cosmic chess. I find myself intrigued by the opportunities such an artifact presents."

Cassandra nodded, understanding the weight behind his words. "Indeed, the balance of power has shifted. The protectors of the artifact—Vikram Nair and his team—have proven formidable. They are bound by ancient oaths but also by something more profound: their connection to each other."

Aditya's eyes narrowed slightly, a glimmer of curiosity sparking within. "Vikram Nair … the one they call Vasuki. A deity in human form, unaware of his full potential until recently. He is an intriguing figure."

Cassandra leaned forward, her interest piqued. "You believe he poses a threat to your plans?"

Aditya chuckled, a deep, resonant sound that filled the room. "Not a threat, Cassandra. An opportunity. Vasuki's return signifies the awakening of ancient forces. His team's dedication to protecting knowledge and their unwavering resolve is admirable, but it also leaves them vulnerable to more strategic players."

Cassandra's eyes sparkled with intrigue. "And you intend to be one of those players?"

Aditya's smile was enigmatic, a blend of charm and cunning. "In the game of power, one must always anticipate the moves of others while concealing one's own. My interest lies in the potential of such forces—how they can be harnessed, understood, and perhaps guided to achieve greater harmony and prosperity."

"Guided?" Cassandra echoed, the skepticism in her voice barely concealed. "You mean controlled."

"Perhaps," Aditya admitted, sipping his cognac with measured ease. "Control is an art, Cassandra. It is about persuasion, alignment of interests, and, sometimes, subtle manipulation. Those who wield power effectively do so with precision and foresight."

Cassandra paused, weighing his words with care, recognizing the layers of strategy and intent that shaped Aditya's perspective. Her ambitions often aligned with his, but she knew that in their world, alliances were as changeable as water.

"There's also the matter of the new variables in play," Cassandra continued, shifting the conversation slightly. "The awakening of these ancient energies has drawn attention from other realms and factions."

Aditya nodded, his gaze intense. "Indeed, the world is on the brink of transformation. But transformation requires visionaries who can navigate the chaos and seize the opportunities it presents. We must be those visionaries, Cassandra."

Their conversation flowed seamlessly through the depths of ancient lore, modern politics, and the complex web of power dynamics. Aditya spoke with the authority of a man who had seen empires rise and crumble, his words carrying the weight of his calculated ambition.

As the night stretched on, the city lights below flickered with an almost living energy, echoing the relentless drive of New York itself. Cassandra and Aditya's exchange was a delicate dance of diplomacy and intrigue, each probing the other's motives while carefully weaving a web of shared interests and the possibility of collaboration.

When Cassandra finally rose to leave, Aditya accompanied her to the elevator, his parting words laden with unspoken promises and carefully veiled challenges. "I look forward to our continued collaboration, Cassandra," Aditya said, his voice smooth and reassuring. "Together, we can shape the narrative of this new era, ensuring that the future aligns with our vision."

Cassandra nodded, a hint of a smile on her lips. "Indeed, Mr. Varun. The game is far from over, and I'm eager to see how it unfolds."

As the elevator doors slid shut, Aditya returned to the solitude of his penthouse, his mind already racing through the complex web of possibilities that lay ahead. The battle for power and influence was far from over, and as a new chapter began to unfold, he knew he would be at the heart of it all, playing a pivotal role in the shifting narrative.

Meanwhile, across the city, a small group of protectors gathered in a cozy café, a quiet retreat from the chaos of recent events. Vikram Nair, now fully connected to his true identity as Vasuki, sat at a table with his team: Maya Singh, Rohan Patel, Anjali Kapoor, and Raj Mehta.

The café was a cozy retreat, its walls lined with photographs and paintings that captured a rich cultural history. The air was thick with the comforting scent of freshly brewed coffee, and soft conversations from other patrons filled the background. It was a peaceful sanctuary amidst the city's chaos, a space where the team could pause and reflect on their shared journey.

As Vikram took a sip of his coffee, his mind wandered to the lessons they had learned along the way. The fight to protect the artifact had pushed them to their limits, but it had also uncovered deeper truths about their world. Ancient forces still stirred beneath the veneer of modern life, and the choices they made now would shape the future in ways they couldn't yet fully grasp.

Vikram's eyes met Maya's, and in that brief moment, an unspoken understanding passed between them. Their shared experiences had created a bond that went beyond the challenges they had faced. Maya's unwavering support and wisdom had been his steadying force, and in her presence, he found both comfort and strength.

"Thank you, Maya," Vikram said softly, his voice filled with genuine emotion. "For everything. Your courage and insight have been a guiding light through the darkest moments."

Maya smiled, her eyes reflecting a deep affection. "We've faced the impossible together, Vikram. And I've always believed in you—in Vasuki. Your journey is just beginning, and I'm honored to be part of it."

Anjali looked up from her notes, her analytical demeanor giving way to a rare smile. "Indeed, Vikram. The knowledge we've uncovered, the mysteries we've solved—they're just the beginning. There's so much more to explore and understand."

Rohan chimed in, his playful enthusiasm infectious. "And with our combined skills, we're unstoppable! The world better watch out—we're just getting started."

Raj nodded in agreement, his voice steady and sincere. "Together, we've proven that unity and purpose can overcome even the most daunting challenges. We've made a difference."

As the conversation continued, the group turned their attention to the future—the challenges they expected and the opportunities that lay ahead. They talked through new strategies, possible allies, and the need for constant vigilance in a world where shadows and secrets were always intertwined.

Vikram's thoughts often wandered back to Aditya Varun, whose influence hung over the situation like an enigmatic presence. The business tycoon's growing interest in the mystical world was a puzzle that couldn't be ignored, one that would require careful thought and strategic moves to navigate.

Maya sensed Vikram's introspection and placed a reassuring hand on his arm. "Aditya Varun is a formidable player, but we've faced formidable foes before. We'll be ready for whatever comes."

Vikram nodded, the resolve in his heart matched by the determination in his eyes. "Yes, we will. We've been entrusted with the knowledge and power of ancient forces, and it's our duty to protect them—and the world—from those who would misuse them."

As the group continued to strategize, sharing memories and dreams, the café became a quiet sanctuary of hope and purpose. Outside, the city carried on with its relentless pace, unaware of the extraordinary journey unfolding within its walls.

In that moment of reflection and camaraderie, Vikram realized that their struggle had created something lasting—a legacy of unity, courage, and resilience that would carry them forward into whatever the future held.

As the night grew deeper and the stars shimmered like distant echoes of forgotten myths, the team readied themselves for the next chapter of their journey. The world lay before them, a vast tapestry of potential, and they were its weavers—connected by fate, driven by purpose, and guided by the timeless light of ancient wisdom.

As the group gradually parted ways, each of them carrying the weight of their shared experiences and renewed determination, Vikram and Maya stayed behind for a moment longer. The city lights stretched out before them, painting a picture of dreams and endless possibilities, and the air seemed to hum with the promise of a fresh start.

Vikram turned to Maya, his gaze soft yet unwavering. "We've come a long way, Maya. And I know there's much more to do. But with you by my side, I feel ready to face whatever challenges lie ahead."

Maya smiled, her eyes reflecting a deep sense of contentment. "Together, we're unstoppable, Vikram. Whatever the future holds, we'll meet it with courage and love."

Their hands intertwined, a silent testament to the bond that had blossomed between them—born from adversity and strengthened by love and a shared sense of purpose.

As they walked into the night, their hearts filled with hope and resolve, the city around them seemed to welcome them, reflecting the unwavering spirit of those who dared to dream and fight for a better tomorrow.

Meanwhile, across the city, Aditya Varun sat alone in his office, a place steeped in shadows and secrets. The events of the day weighed on his mind, stoking the fire of his resolve to reshape the world according to his vision.

The office was a study in contrasts—a mix of luxury and understated elegance, with dark wood furnishings and rich tapestries lining the walls. A large map covered one wall, its surface dotted with strategic points and pathways, hinting at secret plans and far-reaching ambitions.

Aditya sat back in his chair, his eyes locked on the map. His empire was vast, his influence undeniable, but he knew the game was far from over. The events surrounding the artifact had only marked the beginning of a new era, where ancient forces and modern ambitions would inevitably collide.

His mind drifted to Vasuki, the deity in human form who had proven to be both a challenge and a chance. The protectors of the artifact were powerful, but Aditya saw an opportunity—alliances to forge influence to gain, and a way to shift the balance in his favor.

As he mulled over the possibilities, a soft knock at the door broke his thoughts. He turned to find his most trusted advisor, Julian Blackwood, stepping into the room.

"Julian," Aditya greeted, his voice a smooth blend of authority and intrigue. "I assume you've been keeping an eye on our interests?"

Julian nodded, his demeanor as composed as ever. "Indeed, Mr. Varun. The protectors have proven resilient, but their paths are not without vulnerabilities. Our strategies remain adaptable, and our resources are formidable."

Aditya's smile was one of satisfaction. "Good. The world is a canvas of potential, and we are the artists who will shape its future. The key is to remain vigilant and decisive, seizing opportunities and neutralizing threats."

Julian regarded Aditya with a mixture of respect and admiration. "You've always had a keen eye for the bigger picture, Mr. Varun. The challenges ahead are significant, but with your leadership, our ambitions will be realized."

As Julian left, Aditya's gaze returned to the map, his eyes alight with ambition and determination. The future was a puzzle, a tapestry yet to be woven, and he knew he was about to play a key role in shaping its story.

The battle for power and influence was far from over, and with the shadows of the city stretching out before him, Aditya Varun readied himself to navigate the complex web of possibilities that awaited. The world was his stage, and the future called to him, filled with both promise and danger.

With every decision and calculated move, Aditya knew he could shape the narrative, keeping the balance of power tilted in his favor. The past had paved the way, but the future was his to write—a tale of ambition, destiny, and the relentless pursuit of control.

In the grand theater of New York City, where ancient forces and modern ambitions collided, the protectors and power seekers were ready for the next chapter of their intertwined journey. The city's pulse seemed to beat with the promise of fresh challenges and opportunities, its streets a maze of dreams and realities.

Vikram Nair, fully embracing his role as Vasuki, stood at the crossroads of history and destiny, ready to lead his team through the next chapter of their lives. The bonds they had built, the battles they had fought, were not the end but the beginning of a new era—one where ancient wisdom and modern innovation would merge in harmony.

As the night grew deeper, the stars above silently watched over the unfolding story—a tale of courage, love, and the timeless dance between power and responsibility. The world was vast, its mysteries endless, and for those bold enough to dream and fight for a better future, the journey was only just beginning.

In the shadows of the city and under the glow of the stars, the protectors and power seekers readied themselves for the next chapter of their shared journey. The future lay ahead, brimming with possibility and promise, and as dawn neared, the world seemed to hold its breath, waiting for the stories yet to unfold.